Lucy Bethia Walford

A little legacy and other stories

Lucy Bethia Walford

A little legacy and other stories

ISBN/EAN: 9783744751049

Printed in Europe, USA, Canada, Australia, Japan

Cover: Foto ©Andreas Hilbeck / pixelio.de

More available books at **www.hansebooks.com**

A
LITTLE LEGACY

&

OTHER STORIES

BY

MRS. L. B. WALFORD

HERBERT S. STONE AND COMPANY
CHICAGO AND NEW YORK
MDCCCXCIX

CONTENTS

THE LITTLE LEGACY

The Little Legacy

"Wealth often sowes in keeping."
　　　　　　　—QUARLES.

"A hundred thousand is such a good round sum," said Mr. Mapleson, tentatively. "Seems a pity to spoil the symmetry of it, eh? Any little odds and ends that might be over" —and he looked at his client, as though feeling his way, with the caution habitual to a confidential adviser upon delicate ground.

"It might be more than odds and ends," replied the client.

"Of course—of course. Might run up to another 'century,' or—to anything you please. But as it stands you wish to leave a hundred thou-sand—the amount of your actual capital at the present moment—to

3

your nearest of kin, Mr. Charles Grenoble; and there are a few hundreds over——"

"A thousand," corrected the client.

"A thousand. And there may be a few more thousands—there *may* be, as I said, anything you like to name. Should it amount to any decent sum—say, to ten or twenty—nothing would be easier than to add this on; but meantime—hum, ha—is there no one? Have you no poor devil of a relation to whom such a trifle——"

"You have some one in your eye." Mr. Grenoble, the Mr. Grenoble whose will was being made, was a man of quick intelligence, and knew his old friend in and out. "Out with it, Mapleson. Of whom are you thinking?"

"Ha! ha! ha! 'Pon my word——" the lawyer laughed, played with his pen, and shot a glance. He had not meant to be detected in a stray impulse; and, moreover, was not precisely sure whether detection might not defeat his object. "You are so uncommonly sharp," he murmured, "that — well — it's no use beating about the bush with *you;* I had best own up, I suppose: there is that poor fellow, Tom Hathaway——"

"Oh, bother Tom Hathaway!"

"He is some sort of cousin, isn't he?"

"Cousin? What's a cousin?" The rich Mr. Grenoble frowned and growled over his basin of soup. He was an invalid for the time being, and had summoned his solicitor to his sick-room, having, as he said, a day or two leisure wherein to look into his affairs.

"If one were to take into consideration every poor, shiftless hanger-on who calls himself a cousin——"

"Quite so, quite so. It is simply

folly to fritter away capital in driblets. I catch your meaning; and we are quite at one on the point. Still"—the lawyer yawned and shifted his leg—"still, Tom is a decent fellow; and I fancy, with a wife and a large family, must find it rather a struggle——"

"What business has a man in his position with a wife and a large family?"

"None whatever, of course," said Mr. Mapleson, cheerfully. "You and I, two jolly bachelors——" and he proceeded to enlarge.

It took an hour's time, but ere the close of the interview he had gained his point. For each objection raised he had a cordial assent; in all general condemnation of poor men, and the desirability of ignoring their existence, and leaving them to lie upon the bed themselves had made, he could promptly acquiesce; but insensibly the wealthy testator found himself being led, first to argue the pros and cons of the case in question, then to yield a sort of tacit consent, fenced in by many a reservation; and finally to permit the clause to be added which his legal adviser had intended to add from the beginning of the conversation.

"Now, what on earth did I do that for?" muttered the latter to himself as, the business concluded, he went his way. "It has cost me a lot of time and trouble; and, except for the pleasure of getting. my own way, I can't imagine what object I had in view. Benevolence isn't in my line. And it's a queer sort of thing that the sight of a man's face, and a few ordinary words let fall in my hearing—not even addressed to me—should have stirred up all this coil! It's not likely to do any good, either. Grenoble may live for twenty years, and pile up his 'centuries' like W. G. Grace. He will be sending for me again before I can look round, to make a new will, and bowl out poor Tom. Gad! I wish I had let Tom alone! It is two o'clock now," consulting his watch, "and I ought to have lunched at one; and though I told Grenoble that it was no matter, when he was sitting sipping his slops in his comfortable armchair, I didn't bargain for having to go without food until an hour beyond my usual time. What did I do it for, I say?" proceeded the lawyer, testily. "Because I am an old fool, and Tom Hathaway's hungry face—there he is now, coming out of a tea shop!" suddenly bending forward, as his hansom whirled rapidly along the Strand. "Had a roll and butter for his luncheon, I dare say—and some coffee, or disgusting trash of that kind! No wonder he looks white and thin! Digestion all gone to the dogs, I'll be bound. Faith! Tom, if you knew what I've been doing for you just now," apostrophising the unconscious pedestrian who hurried past, and was soon lost in the crowd, "you'd hold your shoulders a little straighter, my man! But it'll all come to nothing —it'll all come to nothing," mused Mr. Herbert Mapleson, his busy mind again at work on contingencies and probabilities. "Tom's little legacy will never come off, I shouldn't mind betting a hundred to one. Lucky he doesn't know of it! 'Blessed are they which expect nothing, for they shall not be disappointed.'" And dismissing the subject from his thoughts, the prosperous man of business settled down to other matters, which demanded the whole of his time and attention until the close of the day.

Nothing was further from his anticipations than to have it recalled within the week—almost, as he declared among his colleagues, before the ink was dry upon the parchment—by the swift development of his old friend's complaint, ending as it did in Mr. Grenoble's decease before the lapse of another month.

"Bless my soul! if Tom Hathaway hasn't come in for that legacy after all! I—'pon my word—I little thought I was doing Tom such a good turn."

It was not perhaps strictly decorous, but this was, as a fact, Mr. Mapleson's first thought on receiving the intelligence.

He had been prepared for it. The doctors had looked serious from the day on which a change set in and new symptoms appeared (that being, as we have said, very shortly after the interview above narrated took place); in consequence our legal friend had had time to acclimatise himself to the idea, and to ponder

at intervals over the contents of the
will which he had so recently drawn
up; also to heave an easy sigh now
and again on the altar of friendship.

But he had never known Mr.
Grenoble intimately; their relations
had always been more or less on a
business footing; and he knew so
many people—met so many familiar
countenances every day—had such
innumerable interests, and such a
cool head and heart wherewith to
meet them—that one loss in the
large circle of his acquaintance—
one, moreover, which did not enter
into his daily life—could not be
expected to affect him deeply.

Furthermore, there was a "big
thing" on the Stock Exchange
which interested Mr. Mapleson very
keenly indeed. He could not quite
make up his mind about it; it might
be that he was losing a chance; on
the other hand, he was disinclined
to meddle with any of his invest-

ments, and had no loose money handy at the moment. He was almost worried about the matter; and had nearly decided to let things go, and turn a deaf ear to the crowings over their luck which fortunate speculators kept pouring into his ear, when the post brought him a large fee which came in a manner unexpectedly—that is to say, he had not reckoned upon its payment before a later date. He took the cheque and looked at it; then he rang the bell. Within half an hour his broker on 'Change had received an order. This was on the day of Mr. Grenoble's demise.

It was a matter of course that Mr. Mapleson should attend the funeral, which followed within the week; and he reflected that after discharging that unpleasant duty—for the day was bitterly cold and raw, and the long, slow drive to Kensal Green, in addition to the rest of the ceremonial, was a detestable prospect—he should at least have some gratification in the two legal communications regarding the nature of the will, which would fall to his pen. One of these, indeed, he dashed off through his clerk as he was putting on his great coat.

"Poor Tom Hathaway will go home a trifle warmer this wretched evening if he carries this note in his waistcoat pocket," reflected he, briskly moving about and turning over papers to make sure that nothing was forgotten.

"I shan't return to the office, Williams," aloud to the confidential clerk. "It will be late before I get back from the cemetery, and Mr. Charles Grenoble may wish me to go with him to his house. But mind that I get all notes and letters which come in before the office closes, as soon afterwards as possible. Bring them to me yourself. And if Mr.

So-and-So should send over (naming his broker), 'go and see him yourself; tell him where I am gone, and if he has any message of importance, ask him either to wire or to give you a note. Prepare the draft for Mr. Charles Grenoble, and bring it to me to sign. I don't think there is anything else;'' and taking up his hat and gloves the speaker, somewhat ruefully, quitted his snug chamber and prepared to brave the raw atmosphere of a November afternoon.

But few of those who had known the late Mr. Grenoble cared to do the same; and it appeared that on the return journey his nephew and only relation present was about to drive alone in the mourning coach which had followed next the hearse in the outward-bound procession, when on a sudden Mr. Mapleson took a resolution. He had been somewhat coldly greeted by the principal mourner, for whom he had neither liking nor esteem—(and it may be added that he had merely thrown in the suggestion of going to Mr. Charles Grenoble's house, above recorded, as an excuse for not returning to the City, rather than from any real intention of carrying it into effect)—but it occurred to him now that it might be rather an amusing experience to try the effect of unbosoming himself regarding the will he had drawn up a month before, when alone with the principal legatee.

"Whatever he may *expect*, he can't be *certain* of anything," reflected the lawyer, shrewdly, "and I should doubt if he even has any great expectations.   There was no love lost between the two.   They kept aloof from each other as much as they could, and snapped and snarled when they had to meet.   They were as like as two peas—a couple of

surly, selfish, ill-conditioned peas.
But 'tis ill speaking hard words of
the dead," hastily covering his head
again, as the group moved away
from the grave. "I oughtn't to
have been thinking of such things
just now," with a twinge of re-
morse, "and perhaps poor Charles
Grenoble," casting a glance in the
latter's direction, "would be hurt
and affronted if he knew. He *may*
have some feeling, for all that stucco
face. Anyhow, he'll look sweet for
once, when he hears he has come in
for a hundred thousand pounds.
That's a lubrication adamant itself
can't resist. He might even give
me some of the handling of it," and
Mr. Mapleson was presently by the
other's side.

"If you have no objection, I shall
ride home with you?" And a somewhat stiff assent having been signi-
fied, the coach started with its two
occupants.

"You will receive a formal communication from me in the course of this evening, Mr. Grenoble." ("May as well begin at once," cogitated the lawyer, feeling that the sooner the ice was broken the better.) Then he emitted a little preliminary cough, and straightened his collar. "I dare say that its contents will be no surprise." Here the speaker paused, awaiting some sign of interest. None came.

"Being the late Mr. Grenoble's natural heir"—(another pause; Mr. Charles Grenoble looked straight in front of him)—"you are, of course, prepared to hear that he has made a will in your favour." Still no response.

("Won't commit himself," muttered Mapleson, internally. "Uncivil brute, as he always was!")

"I drew it up a month ago," proceeded he, aloud, "and am pleased to be able to inform you — (Hanged

if I am pleased!" mental comment)
—"that the amount of your uncle's
capital at that time was a hundred
thousand pounds; which sum is left
to you unconditionally. Your uncle
was worth a hundred thousand odd,
I should say—for there was a trifle
over, how much I don't quite know
—bequeathed to another and more
distant relation."

"To whom?" For the first time
the fixed, immovable lips parted;
but the head did not turn—no,
not by a hair's breadth—towards
Mr. Charles Grenoble's companion.

"To whom? To your cousin, Mr.
Thomas Hathaway. Mr. Hathaway——"

"I have no interest in Mr. Hathaway."

"Ah, indeed; no family inter-
course. Yes, I suppose so; I
understood as much; but Mr.
Grenoble thought——"

A wave of the other's hand disposed of Mr. Grenoble's thoughts.

("What on earth—is he not going
to say *anything?* Was there ever
such a—— Confound it! I wish I
had not let myself in for this! Devil
take him and his hundred thousand!") The lawyer's temper was
rising; Mr. Mapleson was not a man
to be treated with indignity; and the
present rebuff was the more acutely
felt in that he had prepared himself
for something altogether different.

He would have had no objection to
a passage at arms with Mr. Charles
Grenoble at any time; even coldness
and silence could have had their tit-
for-tat on any other occasion. But
to have somewhat genially broached
a subject, confident of its favourable
reception, one which should have
obtained at least a civil hearing, and
display of interest, if not of warmth
—and to have been snubbed—yes,
actually snubbed—as though he had

made an officious and altogether superfluous communication, was intolerable.

He drew himself upright in his corner, vowing inwardly that he had learned a lesson in mankind. Even the acquisition of a hundred thou-sand pounds would not make a cur less a cur for a single fraction of a minute, than he was by nature.

Certes, if silence were the order of the day, he would not again essay to break it. He too could look gloomily out of his window, and occupy himself with his own reflec-tions.

He had enough to think about, in all conscience. Perhaps at that very time he was making a handsome *coup* on 'Change, one which should bring him in, if not a hundred thou-sand, at any rate what would be a very solid addition to his already flourishing income. He would be pleased enough to net his six or seven thousand, and would not be above owning it. Indeed, he frankly avowed to himself that the telling his friends, and chuckling over his good fortune with them, would be the "milk in the cocoanut" of the whole proceeding.

Mr. Mapleson was not an avaricious man, and had already all his wants supplied, together with a future comfortably provided for. But it was his theory that no man of sense ever despised wealth; and since he himself was ready to acknowledge this opinion—to proclaim and justify it, if need were—it was unendurable in his eyes that a professed money-grubber, such as he had always held Mr. Charles Grenoble to be, should stroke his impassive face and stare vacantly from the window, affecting indifference to the important news he had just heard. Worse than all, that he should have the cool audacity to imagine that anyone, least of all his clever self, could be deceived by such a clumsy piece of acting.

As soon as decency permitted, he would end the scene and escape from the thrall of such companionship—never, he swore to himself, to be caught in such a trap again—and accordingly hailed a passing hansom, the first that came in sight.

"You are getting out here?" Mr. Charles Grenoble involuntarily exhibited participation in the other's relief; then, to the lawyer's amazement, held out his hand with actual and undisguised cordiality. "Stop one moment, Mr. Mapleson, before you get out. I believe I ought to beg your pardon for having been rude to you just now. I am afraid you must have thought my conduct somewhat extraordinary, but I assure you it was not intentional—that is to say, the fact is I am so

bothered with money coming in
from here and from there, and from
goodness knows where, that sometimes I"—(putting his hand to his
forehead)—"the worry of it will
drive me distracted some day, I
believe! I was just afraid of what
my uncle would do. Of course, he
could not leave it to anyone else;
that would have been highly im-
proper; and I can't imagine what
could have put it into his head to
throw any away upon that poor,
unfortunate Tom Hathaway, who
has never *got on* in anything he
undertook, has never been the
slightest credit to the family, and
has not been taken any notice of by
either of us for years and years.
To rake him up now is a sheer piece
of folly, and will lead to endless com-
plications. He will fancy he is to
begin coming to our houses, and will
be expecting invitations and so forth
—and this when he has been kept at

arm's length all his life! There was
no need to have disturbed the exist-
ing state of things—none whatever.
I must own, Mr. Mapleson, that for
a moment I had a sort of suspicion
that it was you who had been so
inconsiderate as to prompt my
uncle"—(if Mr. Mapleson experienced any internal sensations, at
least he did not betray himself)—
"and that annoyed me," proceeded
the speaker, as though now satisfied
he had made a wrongful accusation.
"The whole thing is annoying; but
I must do my best," heaving a sigh.
"I must look out some new invest-
ments, and go through those the
funds are in already. It will be a
heap of trouble—endless trouble—
and that just when I was hoping to
take things a little more easily. My
doctor says that if I don't take care
and give myself more holiday, he
won't answer for the consequences.
Look at my poor uncle! And I

have double, treble his responsibilities. I have nearly double as much again to manipulate; it's a heavy strain upon a man. I ask you, therefore, to excuse me, Mr. Mapleson, if in the first flush of vexation I could not bring myself to acquiesce cordially in the arrangement. I hope you will overlook anything that gave you offence, and —and I shall communicate with you later on."

"Now, how much of that was genuine, and how much was humbug?" quoth Mapleson to himself, trying to get over his first surprise. "There was *some* truth in it, but there was a lot of sham. He does grudge the trouble; but he wouldn't let go *one stiver* of the money—no, not even Tom Hathaway's poor little popgun of a legacy, if by hook or by crook he could have collared it too!"

.   .   .   .

"Oh, do, Jenny, not heap up such

an enormous fire, and knock the ashes about all over the place!"

Jenny's mamma spoke with a fretful intonation, which was obviously foreign to her nature and quickly repented of. "I know you mean well, my dear; and it is nice for your father to see a bright fire and a clean hearth when he comes in—especially on a night like this," glancing outside, for the shutters were not yet shut, and the street lamp opposite the window revealed the raw, murky atmosphere and reeking damp of a November evening — "but there's no need to waste——"

"I didn't mean to waste at all." Jenny, a tall girl of fifteen, plied tongs and shovel vigorously. "I shan't waste a single cinder; they shall all go on the top," protested she, suiting the action to the word. "But I know poor papa will come in cold and miserable, and you always tell me to make the room look comfortable for him—to cheer him up and give him a welcome. I thought you liked a good fire," in aggrieved accents.

"Yes—yes, my dear—yes, of course; I am not blaming you, only coals are such a terrible price; here is an enormous bill just come in;" the speaker sighed and glanced at a paper in her hands. "How it is ever to be paid, I am sure I don't know!"

"But you knew it had to come, mamma."

"I knew; but I hoped to get some others settled first. There are several that I have been keeping back; thinking that, as this was the last day of the month, your father would get his salary paid and I could ask him to let me have the money."

"Well, can't you, and leave the coals for a little longer?"

"Oh, yes, I *can;* in fact, I *must*"—again the speaker sighed and looked dejectedly round—"but I could hardly bear to see that great cart-load at the door to-day, just when the cook was telling me that she must have the plumber sent for to the kitchen range, and that something has gone wrong with the tap in the scullery too."

The door opened and another daughter entered.

"What a comfort to see a decent fire!" exclaimed she, popping down upon a stool in front. "I am so cold in this thin frock. Mamma, I suppose we may send for patterns of warm things now, mayn't we? You said if we hung on till the end of November we could get our winter frocks in time for Christmas. And I have been thinking——"

"Do you suppose you really must have them? There are so many of you, if we once begin; and now that skirts are so wide they take such yards and yards of material——"

"I was going to say," said Bertha, looking thoughtfully into the fire, "that if we could have some stuff for new blouses—some really good, nice-looking, warm material, velveteen or corduroy——"

"Corduroy is very expensive," interpolated her mother.

"It would be nothing compared with the expense of coats and skirts such as other girls have. And we might manage to make our old skirts do by lining them with flannel or flannelette."

"Oh, Bertha, mine could *never* do." The younger and less considerate Jenny rushed into the arena with a terrified protest. "Mine is all stained and frayed," cried she, exhibiting here and there the deficiencies indicated.

But Bertha was resolute. "It could be turned," said she,

decidedly. "You could help to do it
yourself, if we had some one in to
make the blouses; we could easily
work under her direction. But,
mamma," in a lower voice, "I am
afraid the little ones really must
have some new underclothing. You
know how Wynnie has been cough-
ing all this week, and when I went
into the nursery this morning, Jane
told me she did not like to worry
you, but that she was sure both the
children were not properly clothed
for this weather. She showed me
their things——"

"They shall have what they
require; I shall manage it somehow," said Mrs. Hathaway, hurriedly; "I have still something to
sell," involuntarily turning round
the diamond ring upon her finger.
"Bertha—Jenny—not a word to your
father—nor to the boys—nor anyone. At least we can spare them
this. And if I should get enough,"

looking fondly at her sole ornament, "for you, my poor dears, to have—-"

"Never mind *us*." Bertha came and threw herself across her mother's knees. "We can do very well. I didn't know it was as bad as that, mamma; only the poor children——"

"Yes, yes; you were quite right to tell me about them. If I were able to go into the nursery myself! But no one must think of keeping things back from me because of my being an invalid. It would make me worse —far worse—than anything else, to know that others were suffering from my neglect."

"Neglect! You did everything in the world for us as long as you could," said Bertha, in a choking voice, whilst Jenny, subdued, also leant tearfully against her mother's chair. "You worked and slaved for us," continued the elder girl, with breath coming and going fast, "sit-

ting up at nights, and staying at
home all the fine summer days, and
never taking a holiday, and always
pretending that you were so well
and strong, until you could pretend
no longer——"

"Hush! hush! There is your
father at the gate." Mrs. Hatha.
way, who had been returning
tenderly the kisses pressed upon her
cheek, suddenly started upright, and
dashed the moisture from her eyes.
"He must not find us like this,"
said she, briskly. "There is little
enough in his own life to cheer and
encourage him; and if he finds us
down it will depress him the more,
and unfit him for doing the work he
has to do. He often has a headache
when he comes in. That's right,
Bertha, go out and meet him; and,
Jenny, dear, try not to bring forward unpleasant subjects; you know
what I mean. You have not quite
Bertha's tact, though I know your

dear, warm heart would not for the world give anyone pain.''

''But, mamma, is there any use in shirking?''

Mrs. Hathaway held up a warning finger, for the tones of a shrill young voice were somewhat .too penetrating, and the front door had now admitted the master of the household.

Then the mother replied in a firm, steady undertone, ''There *is* no use in 'shirking'—but neither is there any use in discussions which cannot further the object in view. When there is anything to be *done*, it would be foolish and cowardly, it would be wrong, to shrink from speaking out and taking counsel together; but merely to bewail our poverty, and indulge in useless aspirations and enumerations of things we need which we cannot get, and must learn to do without, is but waste of breath, and worse. By overshadowing our spirits, and turning our thoughts downwards instead of upwards, this kind of talk interferes with our going through our daily work diligently, and meeting our troubles cheerfully. Now, run out and see what they are waiting in the hall for," proceeded the invalid, in a lighter tone; for Mrs. Hathaway was, for the time being, chained to the little hard couch which did duty for a sofa in her small, plainly-furnished drawing-room.

Mrs. Hathaway was one who practised what she preached, and in the few moments which elapsed ere figures were again seen in the doorway she had gathered strength from no unfamiliar Source, and composed her features to their usual gentle air of serenity and welcome.

She had made up her mind that the day had dragged as heavily with her husband as with herself.

It had been an especially trying

one from various points of view in the humble household. We have had a glimpse of its culminating scene; and there had been divers lesser annoyances to contend with, some of one sort, some of another; while, through all, there had grated harshly on the sensitive nerves of the poor prisoner, who could never escape out of hearing, the scrunching and snorting of a loathsome steam roller, which ground endlessly up and down over the newly-repaired suburban road in front.

Even her gentle soul had been stung to irritation at last, as we know, and the goodly hotbed of coals with which the small apartment was now glowing had nearly had their flames quenched by her at the outset.

That had passed, and she was now glad they were there; glad that her poor husband, coming in weary and chilled—too often downcast and dispirited also—but how was this?

It was certainly no downcast, dispirited countenance which met her timorous, faintly-investigating smile. It was a voice most unlike her poor Tom's usually subdued tones—(poor fellow! he had almost forgotten how to speak jovially)—which responded to her wifely inquiries. It was a brisk, alert, upright little grey-headed man who stepped into the room, and who laughingly threw off a couple of excited girls eagerly clamouring for the problem to be unravelled, and the secret, whose existence had been admitted, to be disclosed in the hearing of all.

"You shall hear it, sure enough." The father and husband bent over the sofa for the never-failing embrace. "Jenny, love" — in his excitement the old name, which had of late been transferred to the younger proprietor, rose to Mr. Hathaway's lips; and he stroked fondly the head that had once been as glossy and golden as the other Jenny's was now—"I have brought home a medicine that will go far to cure thy ailment, poor wifie," and the speaker sat down beside the couch, and held out his other hand to the two impatient ones standing by.

At the same moment a boy burst in, laden with school books. Quick as thought, Bertha had turned round with an imperative sign, and opened her mouth to bid the intruder retire, when, "No, no," cried her father, beckoning Charlie also within the circle; "come in, my boy, come in. I've got a bit of good news to tell, and you shall hear it with the rest." Then he paused and looked solemnly, yet with radiance shining in his eyes, at each in turn. "A wonderful thing has happened," he said, "a most extraordinary and—and wonderful thing. I have

been left a legacy of a thousand
pounds!''

.   .   .   .

"There seems no end to what it
will do," cried Bertha, over and
over again.

Twenty-four hours had passed,
and each had been filled with its
own measure of joyful communings
and glad anticipations.

"Mamma, to think how nearly
you had lost *that!*" continued the
affectionate girl, touching the beautiful ring, whose diamonds seemed
to emit a new effulgence—as indeed
they did, for nothing would serve
the enthusiastic Jenny but to clean
and brighten them afresh in honour
of the occasion. "Oh, mamma, perhaps only another day and it would
have gone! The one jewel you
possess in the world! And what we
all know you value besides, because
of so many associations. . . .
Well, now, I have made out the list

of bills," and with tenfold the importance of a judge Bertha spread her papers, pencil in hand, "and we will pay every one of them first of all. They don't amount to much in the light of a thousand pounds," continued she, joyously, "although they seemed so overwhelming when we had only poor papa's salary to go upon, and they were to be scrimped one by one out of every month as it came in. Perhaps we may not even need to touch the thousand at all for the bills; as Mr. Mapleson wrote that there was a thousand 'odd,' and that 'odd' may quite likely cover the bills, papa thinks. And then we may use a hundred, may we not, in getting put to rights altogether? The house really wants it *dreadfully*——"

"Indeed, it does." But Mrs. Hathaway's acquiescence was rather one of pleased anticipation than of regret. "It ought to have been

painted from top to bottom last
year.   And had it not been our own
we should have been forced to do it;
no landlord would have let us off.
We thought that was the one good
thing about our having bought this
poor little house and mortgaged it so
heavily.   We shall pay off the mort-
gage now,'' and she looked round
with the air of a proud proprietor.
"You must remember, children, that
we shall not receive Mr. Grenoble's
legacy at once; and though your
father will have no difficulty in getting an advance on the security of
Mr. Mapleson's letter, it will only
be a few hundreds.   Still, a few
hundreds, and the rest to follow
shortly!''—and her eyes shone.

"I was thinking we really ought
to have a little household linen,''
meditated Bertha aloud.   "The
towels are so very thin, and there
are hardly enough to go round——''

"And the water-cans are in a

deplorable state,'' assented her mother.

"And, oh, mamma, can't we have the piano tuned?" It was Jenny's turn next. "The tuner has not been here since April.''

"You may send for him at once;'' Mrs. Hathaway nodded cheerfully. "And poor Charlie's bed, I will have that mended. The poor boy never complains, but it must have been very uncomfortable. And the lock of his door is broken—Oh, there is your father's voice outside!'' All paused to listen. "He has brought some one home with him,'' said Mrs. Hathaway, with a fresh smile. "He used often to bring a friend home in this easy way when we were first married; but it is so long since we have had anything to offer. That's right, Bertha, make a blaze,'' and she drew herself up on the couch, and arranged the coverlet over her feet to prepare for company.

She was hardly prepared, however, for the visitor who was ushered in. Although she knew Mr. Mapleson, she had not seen him hitherto within the walls of her own modest dwelling. Here also was a new departure.

"Mr. Mapleson was good enough to say he would come down with me and call upon you this evening, my dear." It was natural that the speaker's accents should have in them a certain formality in the presence of a stranger, but it did not escape the wife's ear that there was also a nervous intonation and something of the well-known shadow on her husband's brow. He now proceeded.

"Mr. Mapleson wished to consult with us both on a little matter of business——"

"An investment for the legacy left you by the terms of Mr. Grenoble's will;" the lawyer took up the thread, and seated himself with a courteous inclination towards the young lady who had hastened to place a chair.

"An investment?" Mrs. Hathaway looked from one to the other with feminine appeal for enlightenment.

"My wife does not understand much about such things; neither, to tell the truth, do I." Mr. Hathaway forced a little laugh, which had not a genuine ring. "We did not quite understand, did we, my dear? that this money which our cousin has been kind enough to leave us has to be invested—will remain in Mr. Mapleson's charge, to be invested for us—so we shall get the interest instead of the capital. Of course, it's all right; no doubt it is better so; it will last longer, and——"

"But perhaps it is a little disappointment?" The visitor looked keenly round. "I dare say the ladies have already spent in imagination——"

"That's it; just so." The girls' father made a hasty movement, as though to intervene between their faces and the guest. "I was a little over-hasty in telling them; and they had been reckoning up, as young people will—but, of course, *we* understand," and the poor little man made a dignified movement and straightened himself upon the hearthrug.

"Yes, *we* understand." The voice from the sofa was low and soft, but no tremor was audible. ("A woman who would back up her husband in anything," decided Mr. Mapleson within himself.) "We are greatly obliged to you for taking this trouble," continued the speaker, steadily, "and shall be very glad of any help you can give us."

Mr. Mapleson produced some papers from his pocket. As he did so he heard a husky whisper behind his chair.

"Are we not to get *any* of it now,
Bertha?"   And looking up at the
same moment the quick-witted lawyer perceived a spasm upon the
father's face, and noted that the
mother had averted hers.

When they spoke, however, no one
would have guessed the effort which
shaped the syllables of calm propriety which fell from the elder's
lips.   The papers were passed from
one to the other.   Mr. Mapleson's
proposals were hearkened to with
deference; his advice was taken,
and himself empowered to act in all
respects according to his own judgment.

Still he did not go; he seemed
unwilling to go.   He entered into a
discussion about the merits, or
demerits, of the neighbourhood; his
eye wandered round and round the
little room, taking in—or at least so
poor Bertha fancied—the shabby,
darned curtains and broken window-

cord; and though there was more than one prolonged pause, it was not until all had begun to feel the strain almost beyond their powers to bear, that he at length rose.

"You won't stay to dine with us?" said Mr. Hathaway, faintly. He knew there would be a good dinner—the dinner which had been ordered to celebrate the family festival—and hospitality prompted the invitation, even while a sick sinking at the heart almost forbade its utterance.

All the glorious news of yesterday seemed to have turned to a mirage. It was true that forty pounds a year, which Mr. Mapleson considered would be the probable interest of the sum bequeathed, meant a pleasing addition to his annual income. But compared with a thousand pounds down!

The "odd," too, had faded out of sight. It had only amounted to a trifle, and had been used for expenses. He was longing to be rid of another presence, yet shrank from the moment when he and his should be again alone. How happily had he gone forth that morning! How smoothly had the wheels of life rolled throughout the day! And how confidently had he awaited the glad bustle of his return!

It had been agreed that a family conclave was to be held, and pros and cons discussed. He could scarcely bear to mark the quietude of the little chamber now.

"Just step with me a moment outside, will you?" said Mr. Mapleson.

.   .   .   .

"But, my dear sir, I—I, really—I am so bewildered! This munificence —this extraordinary, unparalleled good fortune!" Poor Tom Hathaway shook all over, and a narrow slip of paper in his hand wriggled in the lamplight. "It is incredible—"

"Not at all incredible." A hearty
hand patted him on the shoulder.
"You think me a cold-blooded indi-
vidual, Hathaway; and I dare say
wouldn't give me credit for—but
even a selfish old bachelor may
sometimes enjoy giving a pleasant
surprise. I didn't come all this way
out to shed gloom and disappointment in a place that, to tell the
truth, looks dismal enough without
the need of anything additional,"
with an involuntary glance of dis-
paragement at the sodden road and
monotonous frontage.

("God bless my soul! How can
people live in such a locality?" muttered Mapleson to himself.)

Then he continued his cheerful
strain aloud, "Let me explain. I
meant to have my little joke—to
tease your wife and daughters for a
few minutes, and then to produce
this cheque and make them jump.
But somehow I couldn't do it.

There was *that* in your wife's face—
and those poor girls! Well, well,
forgive my seeing below the surface,
Hathaway; we lawyers can't help
prying, you know; and even your
mask of cheerful acquiescence didn't
take me in.   It was a disappointment, eh? I had guessed as much,
but I didn't know *how* much until—
never mind when.   It made me feel
queer, I can tell you.   Now, my
good sir, do you understand that
this," tapping the cheque, "is your
own earned money—(at least if it
can be called 'earned,'" *sotto voce*).
"Anyhow, it's made honestly,—and
I had nothing to do with it beyond
the fact that I was the medium of
making it for you. Are you listening? I don't suppose you are," jogging his dumb companion playfully
by the elbow. "But still, as you
have got to tell others, you may as
well let me tell you once again. On
the day of Mr. Grenoble's death,.

when I knew you would come in for this small legacy—small as compared with what he left his other relation, that grumbling curmudgeon Charles —the Stock Exchange was 'humming' with African shares. I made up my mind to have a fling on your account; and if it turned up trumps, well and good; if not, I guaranteed in my own mind to make good the loss. I had just done uncommonly well for myself in the same line, and could afford it. That was a week ago, and the result of the week is that your thousand has made five! I retain the original sum, to be invested according to Mr. Grenoble's wishes—(which I explained just now to yourself and Mrs. Hathaway)— and for the other four thousand you hold the cheque in your hands. It is yours absolutely—and you can make ducks and drakes with it as soon as you like. Eh? Oh, never mind. No thanks. God bless you,

my dear fellow; God bless you,"
and with a parting grip of the hand
the speaker vanished in the darkness.

Nor did the worthy Mapleson's
kindness end here. He had received
an impression from the visit never
to be effaced. He took an ever-
increasing interest in the affairs of
the family he had befriended. In
the course of time the schoolboy
Charlie was received into his office;
and one fine day when his nephew
and heir, Herbert Mapleson, came
and stood before him, bristling with
resolution and defiance, to announce
that he had offered his hand and
heart to Bertha Hathaway, and that
neither his people nor hers should
put a spoke in his wheel, for marry
her he would, &c., &c., with all the
usual variations—all the formidable
uncle did was to hear him to the
end, and then say, with a smile
which he could not for the life of
him make sarcastic, "Bless my soul!

young man, do you think because
people wear spectacles that they
can't see an inch beyond their
noses? There; get me my hat; and
we will go off together to call upon
my future niece. I am not such a
fool, Herbert Mapleson, but I can
still admire a pretty girl, and a good
girl, when I see one. I shall have
to make another fling one of these
days on Tom's account," he cogitated. "It all came of that queer
little legacy of his."

A CLERICAL EXTERIOR

A Clerical Exterior

"As for society, my dear fellow, ahem?" said the vicar, significantly. Then he looked at the youthful, serious figure before him, taking in its spare outlines, the slight bend of the neck and the length—the extreme length—of the new black coat. "Ahem!" he repeated. But inwardly he made the swift and cheerful reflection: "Quite presentable, but absolutely indifferent. Full of zeal and visions. An embryo Loyola or Damien, in short!" with a sarcastic quirk of the lip. "I know the cut. At the present moment it suits me down to the ground."

"I am not in the least solicitous about society," said the new curate, with gentle decision.

"No; I thought not.   Society is—
is all very well in its way; but when
a man is beginning his life-work"—
the speaker shot a glance and marked
that it told—"society is more or less
a hindrance.   Later on it is a different matter.   Your object now is to
learn all you can, and do all you can;
and this great teeming parish of
mine, east of the East of London,
will prove, I trust, an excellent master in the lesson.   There is not"—he
paused, then corrected himself—
"there is hardly more than one house
in it to be visited on equal terms."

The curate did not even ask whose
house it was.

A few days later, however, Mr.
Fairclough himself suggested: "I
must take you to call on Lady Margaret Whitmore, Bertram.   Lady
Margaret will expect it.   She is not
only my principal parishioner, but
the largest landowner in the neighbourhood.   An excellent woman—

liberal, benevolent.   We are lucky
in having such a person in this for-
saken—I mean this queer, out-of-
the-way part of the world.   Every
one else who has ever held property
hereabouts has fled the scene; sold
it for building purposes, and made
off to happier hunting-grounds.   The
East End of London is not what you
can call an agreeable vicinity, and
the East End is approaching us
Essex folk at a gallop.   But Lady
Margaret has struck her roots deep,
like one of her own elms—too deep
ever to be torn up; though one day
doubtless she will snap at the stem,
as they occasionally do.   Long may
that day be off!   And meantime I
must take you with me to Garfords,
and present you in due form."

"When shall we go, sir?" inquired
the young man, glancing at a note-
book in his hand.   "I had better
make a note of it——"

"Pooh!   Note!   Come along now,"

cried the vicar, with genial alacrity. " 'Tis a nice day for a walk, and the walk to Garfords is the only decent one in the place."

"I am afraid this afternoon is full already. I had arranged to call at the schools——"

"My dear boy, the schools can wait."

"And to take these papers for the magazine——"

"Put them in your pocket, and if we have time we can hand them in as we return."

"You wished me to see about the special service——"

"Special service be——" Mr. Fairclough choked the word "hanged" in his throat. He was too apt to let fall unclerical expressions. Aloud, he merely remarked: "My dear Bertram, you are quite right, perfectly right, to map out your time and economize it. There is nothing like method, as I always tell my curates; but all the same, there come occasions when method must go to the wall. It does not do to be a slave to red tape," jogging his young disciple's arm playfully. "I had got my day laid out as well as you, but the sun shines, the birds sing, and the upshot is—away with that note-book!" tapping it with his finger. "There is nothing in it that will not keep till to-morrow or next day; and away we go across the fields to the one house in the neighbourhood where there is the prospect of an hour's real enjoyment in the performance of an actual and positive duty visitation."

He seized his large, important, glossy hat with one hand and his silver-headed cane with the other. Bertram put on a smooth black wideawake, and was extracting his umbrella from the stand when Mr. Fairclough, with half-humorous irritation, pushed it back.

"No, no; can't stand that. An umbrella when there is not a cloud in the sky! In the month of June, too! Here," opening a side door, (for the two were standing in the inner hall of the vicarage, a spacious, well-planned building, as many of its kind are in that region), "here, take your choice. Here are sticks of every sort: sticks long, sticks short; sticks lean, sticks stout; sticks rough, sticks smooth! Some of them haven't been used for twenty years or more, but I go on collecting all the same. Aye, that one will suit you, I dare say; and you handle it as though to the manner born. Come, Bertram, I' see you know a good stick. Don't tell me that you prefer to trudge along a country road with that infernal machine, a parson's umbrella."

"No, sir! I—I never walked with an umbrella in my life till I took orders. But I thought——"

the young man smiled suggest-
ively.

"Aye, I know well enough what
you thought;" Mr. Fairclough's eyes
twinkled. "You are not the first.
And, of course, you are quite right
in a way, Bertram; the good folks
down here have a great eye for the
correct clerical exterior, and Lady
Margaret and her daughters especially expect the clergy to be turned
out *de rigueur*. But an umbrella,
you know, an umbrella! The fact
is, an umbrella is my *bête noire*,
Bertram; and to tell the honest
truth, if I dared I'd pitch both it and
that black wide-awake of yours to the
back of beyond, and see my curates
go about clothed like other gentlemen."

"But, sir——"

"Oh, I know it can't be done, and,
after all, it's a trifle, a mere trifle.
Now, then, this way." And cutting
short the discussion wherein he

feared he had been betrayed too far, the older pedestrian hastily opened a side gate, and after the two had passed through, and he had again secured its fastenings, was ready with a fresh topic of conversation. To himself he said, "I must take care not to shock this guileless youth. Suppose he does pin his faith on a coat or a collar, and suppose I have outlived that illusion, he would be none the better suited to this place and the work before him for adopting my views and discarding his own. As long as he does his part, and fights the world, the flesh, and the devil manfully, what odds if he chooses to *look* it in his own way? Lady Margaret, at any rate, will think none the worse of him." And he chatted sociably and pleasantly as they wended their way along.

"And so I needn't have got this beast of a hat after all," said Bertram to himself. "Confound it, and the coat too! If I had only known!"

He had left Oxford one year before, had taken a good degree, and prepared with zest for the life of a hardworking parish clergyman. Of his own free will he had made this choice; had felt called to it; discovered himself suited to it; and from the bottom of his heart desired nothing better than to concentrate his energies and exercise his best powers in the sacred profession. But he was not quite the meek visionary nor the rapt enthusiast imagined by that very muscular Christian, the Rev. Augustus Fairclough.

"Mary, Mary, how exciting! Two men coming up the lane!" exclaimed the younger Miss Whitmore to her sister, as the two sat lazily upon the lawn at Garfords, with a litter of books and magazines around them. "Two men, actually! Who can they be? Who——"

Mary turned her head slowly, almost contemptuously, round. "It never *is* anybody, so what is the use of saying 'Who?' There is only Mr. Fairclough who it *can* be."

"Mr. Fairclough it is. And the new curate, as I'm a—what a pity mamma is out! She is the curate-lover in this house. We must see them though, and do the civil. After all, Mr. Fairclough would never bring any one here who was not passable, barely passable, even to please mamma. He knows what is due to us—to you and me—and that we can't stand grubs, whatever mamma can. I am rather glad we were at home now. We shall see if this new importation is likely to be any sort of good to us. If only he should be up to the mark for a dinner or a dance——"

"Nonsense!" Mary Whitmore made a restive movement. She was out-of-sorts that day; vexed because of a certain disappointment, and disinclined to put up with interruptions of her brooding mood. "As if a curate could be any good in that way!" she said, petulantly. "And you know what they are, as a rule. I don't know how they manage it, but directly they become rectors and vicars they are nice enough, and pleasant enough—but curates!" and her nose went up in the air.

"Still, he might do for a dinner," persisted the younger, "and I don't believe Mr. Fairclough would bring him to call if he would not do for a dinner. You know he has two other inferior creatures he never thinks of bringing."

"Oh, I don't know; they are all alike," said Mary, indifferently.

None of the indifference, however, was apparent when Miss Whitmore arose to greet her visitors. No one could ever accuse Lady Margaret's

daughters of ill-breeding; and certainly neither of the newcomers had
any reason to suppose that they were
grudged their share of the rustling
shade, nor of the luxurious encamp-
ment on the velvet turf, which
seemed created to invite repose.

"I have been telling Mr. Bertram
that this is the one place in the
neighbourhood where you may
imagine yourself a thousand miles
from London," began the vicar, laying down his stick, and spreading
himself out comfortably. "The
peace and stillness of Garfords is the
one soothing oasis in my great be-
wildering desert of a parish. I come
here when I want to forget where I
live. Ah, how sweet those azaleas
smell!" catching a whiff from a
large clump near. "And the lilac
and may too," sniffing about.
"Delicious, the mingling of fra-
grance! And that white broom
sweeping the water!" his eye going

down to a small lake embedded in shrubs. "This is really Paradise," concluded the speaker, taking off his hat, and burrowing down yet deeper in the basket-chair. "Bertram, I told you this was the day for the Garfords, did I not? Young ladies, I trust you will excuse us for breaking in upon the harmony of such an afternoon, but I think you will agree with me that when a man is to see Garfords for the first time, he ought to see it on a day like this? And now," more briskly, "now, pray, what is the news of the outer world? What have you been hearing? What are you reading?" picking up with the ease of friendship the nearest volume, and plunging instantly into a discussion of its merits.

The theme was interesting, and the young lady animated and intelligent. It only needed the murmur of other voices, and the perception that he was not required to stimulate a lagging dialogue on his other hand, to set the good-natured elderly gentleman free to pursue it; and he was presently so entirely absorbed as to forget any responsibility hitherto felt, connected with the visit.

All at once, however, Mr. Fair-clough was startled. A clear, natural, hearty laugh rang out close to his ear. He broke off short in the very middle of a sentence, to turn a pair of round, surprised eyes upon Bertram.

Bertram was sitting upon the edge of his seat twirling his cane between his fingers, and from his parted lips had emanated a sound never heard before by his clerical superior.

There was nothing disagreeable in the laugh; it could not have been termed either impertinent or familiar; but it was undeniably spontaneous, frank, and mirthful; and somehow—though for the life of him

Mr. Fairclough could not have said how—it took him aback. A gentle, hesitating smile was the outside *he* had ever won from this pale-faced student; and though he had been at times a trifle impatient of such pertinacious solemnity, he had been impressed by it, and inclined to consider its effect upon his parishioners as distinctly advantageous.

What then was the meaning of this new departure? He literally stared, and let it be felt that he was staring.

Margaret Whitmore, who had been the cause of the laugh, and whose own merry eyes were dancing, caught her breath and almost, if not actually, apologised. Bertram's cane fell from his hands, and when he had recovered it, there was a suffusion of colour on his cheek which had certainly not been there before.

"I have been telling Mr. Bertram a story of one of our old farm labourers," and the young lady, with somewhat hurried intonation, repeated the story,—but neither she nor her auditors felt moved to more than a mild appreciation of its flavour on this second narration.

"Ha! ha! ha! Very good!" Mr. Fairclough did indeed emit a faint, commendatory chuckle, and proceed to cap the anecdote on the instant, —but, though he was an excellent *raconteur*, and though his *mot* was superior to Miss Margaret's, he felt that he had not obliterated the memory of his own lapse, nor restored the comfortable unanimity which had preceded it.

If he had only had the sense to sit still and keep his ears open! As it was, he was perforce obliged to go on talking for the whole party, since the abashed Bertram could scarce lift up his head again, while Margaret Whitmore looked as if she too had met with a rebuke. Neither recovered entirely throughout the remainder of the call. . . .

"Yes, you were; you were much too free. Mr. Fairclough thought so, and so did I," exclaimed Mary, afterwards. "Talking and laughing like that with a curate! Of course, the poor man had to laugh back—he could not help it—and then you saw the look he got."

"Gracious me! I saw the look, and I could scarcely believe my eyes. I thought it downright cruel; while as for the poor youth, he got as red as a rose. It was the greatest fun!"

"Fun? Nonsense! Mamma would have been very angry. You know how often she has told you not to be familiar all at once with strangers. The only thing that redeemed it was Mr. Fairclough's annoyance, and his look of blank amazement."

"And the dead stop he made," cried Margaret, with intense appreciation. "The sort of 'Good heav-

ens! What-is-going-to-happen-next?'
expression on his face. Oh, it was
glorious!" and she threw herself
back in her chair, twisting her handkerchief into a ball, tossing it into
the air, and catching it again. "I
must prepare a few more such
shocks for our venerable vicar,"
cried she. "I must lay in a store.
After all, why shouldn't a poor
young parson see a joke as well as
other people? At first you may
imagine how furious I was when I
saw you had usurped dear old Mr.
Fairclough, who is always worth
talking to, and left me to struggle
with the other. I, who had never
been to a 'Mothers' meeting' or a
'Work party' in my life! I could
just manage to be interested in
the 'Lending Library,' because I
thought it would be a good thing to
clear the shelves of all our old magazines and useless books, now that we
have got such a lot of new ones. We

want some more room, and there is a
perfect accumulation.   I told the
youth I should look them out and
send them down.   Unhappily, there
are no Lenten services nor anything
of that sort to inquire about just
now, and I could not venture into the
realms of music and the choir boys.
I had a flying shot at the *Parish
Magazine*, but that soon dropped, so
I made the most of the book-lending.
The youth seemed pensively grateful, and we worried out the subject.
You must have heard how solemnly
we conversed.   Then I tried him—
feeling my way—on croquet and
lawn tennis.   If you will believe
me, a spasm of disgust shot across
his face at the words!   At this point
I felt reckless; I let myself loose to
talk as I chose, and would no longer
attempt to adapt my conversation to
my company, as mamma and you
think one ought to do.   I just *gave*
it him!   I told him all we were

doing and all we were going to do. I didn't care whether he liked it or not. Probably he thinks me an appallingly worldly and frivolous young lady. I ran on exactly as if he had been any other young man, and he bent his gentle head and let the torrent flow over it. But when I got to old Trueman's idea of the Jubilee procession, it found the spot, like Homocea. Some time or other, in the Dark Ages, this spiritual being must have known what it was to laugh, and ever since there has been—there must have been—a pent-up laugh somewhere. Mary, do you know, I am rather proud of myself for having pricked that hidden spot."

"I don't know what you are talking about," said Mary, fretfully. "Here is mamma at last. Perhaps ——" She rose from her chair and stood for a moment ruminating.

"Perhaps what?"

"All that we need to say to mamma is that Mr. Fairclough brought the new curate to call, and that he seems gentleman-like." Again she hesitated. "A man of that sort would be so very useful," she murmured, in conclusion.

"And mamma likes them cadaverous," cried Margaret, gaily. "Mamma!" springing forward and getting her voice in first, as the mother's pet had a trick of doing. "Mamma, you're in luck. Mr. Fairclough has got a curate after your own heart. I don't know if he parts his hair down the middle, because he kept on his abomination of a hat all the time he was here, though I am sure he was longing to take it off, as Mr. Fairclough did his. But in every other respect Mary and I can testify that he meets your views, and we foresee that ycu will have him here morning, noon, and night. He is 'just sweet,' as

they say in America. Now, Mary,
tell the truth, is not this Mr. Bertram 'just sweet'?"

Lady Margaret looked from one
daughter to another.

"I passed the gentlemen at the
lodge; I am sorry to have missed
them."

"Of course you are," cried the
irrepressible younger, "but you will
be glad to hear that we did your part
handsomely—gave them tea, cooled
them down, lent the young man a
book, and stuck a flower in the old
one's button-hole."

"Silly child!" But even Lady
Margaret smiled a fond rebuke.
There were few people who could
resist winsome Margaret—least of all
Margaret's mother. She had, however, a word apart with her elder
daughter presently.

"This Mr. Bertram, I suppose you
really did approve of him?"

"There was nothing to disapprove."

"He seemed a gentleman?"

"Oh, yes, a gentleman."

"Well, my dear?"

"Well, mamma, there is nothing more to say."

"Then I shall ask him to dinner at once."

"Ask him as soon as you like; only——"

. "Have you anything whatever against the man?" demanded Lady Margaret, impatiently. "Why can you not be open about it if you have? You may surely speak to me, confide in me."

"I have nothing to confide, and I have nothing against Mr. Bertram whatever—only Margaret is so young and silly." Margaret's mother understood in an instant.

"She might just try to make a fool of the poor man for the fun of it," proceeded the elder sister, now that the ice was broken. "You know how heedless she is. She calls him a 'youth,' but he is older than she, at any rate. And I could not help fancying once or twice that I saw him looking at her. Mamma, it would be a shame to run any risk of turning that poor curate's head, and yet to say anything to Margaret—!'' Finally a plan of campaign was arranged.

By the end of the summer Bertram had become quite an *habitué* of the house, firmly established in the good graces of all, and, as her daughters had predicted, a special favourite with his hostess.

"Yes, I thought you would like him," observed the vicar, complacently, one day. "An excellent fellow, and throws himself into his work like a man. The only fault I have to complain of—if it be a fault, Lady Margaret—is that Bertram does not seem to know what relaxation is! I have suggested his taking a holiday more than once; or even a day or two off,—but he does not see it at all. He will be invaluable to me as the winter comes on; the people adore him already; and I am grateful to you for all the kindness he has met with at Garfords."

"Indeed, Mr. Bertram is quite an acquisition," rejoined Lady Margaret, briskly. "He has come out so wonderfully of late; and though we really do not see very much of him, that only proves that he is, very properly, too much engaged in parish work to have time for dawdling in ladies' drawing-rooms. When we *do* see Mr. Bertram, he is always welcome."

"A good preacher too, I think, Lady Margaret?"

"A remarkably good preacher, Mr. Fairclough." ("A great deal better preacher than you are yourself," reflected the lady, inwardly. She did not over-rate her vicar's powers in that respect.)

"And a good reader, moreover, I think you will also allow?"

"The best reader we have ever had," said Lady Margaret, with animation.

"I am delighted with your approval," said the vicar, rising. "Your judgment was all that I needed to confirm my own. We have got a treasure, and I only hope we shall keep him. Bertram dines with you to-night, he tells me?"

"To meet my future son-in-law, Captain Satterthwayte," said Lady Margaret, shaking hands. "Captain Satterthwayte has just returned from a voyage, and comes to us to-night; and as the young people have not met for some time, I thought it would be more agreeable to have one other gentleman present, so that Margaret and I should not be quite neglected," with a smile. "The marriage will take place, we hope, next month."

"*Who* is to be there?" cried Bertram, with almost a shout, when, in the course of the next hour, the name of Lady Margaret's other guest was casually let fall by his superior.

The tone of his voice recalled something to Mr. Fairclough's ear, and pondering upon it afterwards he knew what that something was; it was the laugh which had startled him out of his equanimity on the lawn at Garfords five months before.

Since then he had, it is true, grown to recognise the fact that Bertram could laugh, even to anticipate with a pleasurable emotion the response which a droll anecdote or lively narration was sure to call forth when the pensive curate was off his guard—when he could be, as it were, surprised into mirth. But Mr. Fairclough had always felt that it required himself as instigator to produce the genial spark. Bertram's present animation was a puzzle not to be solved by a somewhat elaborate and incoherent explanation.

"He is a very good fellow, but certainly he is rather a queer fellow at times," muttered the vicar to himself.

Still queerer would he have thought the young man could he have peeped into the curate's dressing-room as the evening hours drew on.

Bertram was rocking himself to and fro on a little creaking chair that threatened every minute to give way beneath the strain. Coats and waistcoats lay about at random, and the heavy boots, which had just been kicked off, betrayed, by their distance from their owner, the force with which they had been sent flying. The curate's usually sleek brown hair stood on end fierce and rumpled; his hands clasped his knees, and he rocked and groaned in unison.

"Oh, you fool—you fool! You incarnate idiot! You double-distilled idiot, Jack Bertram! To go and let yourself in for this! How are you going to get out of it? You're not going to get out of it at all. . . . You have just *done* for yourself, intolerable jackass that you are!" . . . Another groan and rock. "After all the wear and tear of it, to end in this! And you knew what it must come to—you knew it all along, you tenfold son of a——! . . . Oh, hold your tongue now, and eat your pie, and be hanged to you! . . . It's the end, I tell you— the end. The game's up. You've played it well—too well, by a long chalk. Every week has let you deeper and deeper into the mire, and now—the deluge!"

"Heigho!" With a long sigh the speaker rose at last and walked to

the mirror on the wall. "He said I
had 'the face for it'—and, by Jove!
he was right! Never more so than
to-night! Lady Margaret will press
on me an extra glass of wine, and
implore me to wrap my throat up
from the night air. Mary Whitmore
will condescend to suggest that I
should take the warm side of the
table at dinner—and Margaret?
Margaret will be really anxious, and
give me one of her troubled looks.
Poor darling! She doesn't like it
any more than I do, now. It was
only a joke at the first. Good heavens! why did we let it get into such
deadly earnest? Lady Margaret will
never forgive us—never! And if we
had only not behaved like two
romantic lunatics, we might now
have been as happy as Frank Satterthwayte and his Mary. I can
pitch into Frank, anyway," he
wound up with gloomy vengeance.

The gloom, however, did not

interfere with Mr. Bertram's being turned out faultlessly when, his toilet complete, he betook himself to the house where, according to his own sensations, the bomb was to burst.

He knew his old chum Satterthwayte, knew that it was beyond the power of mortals to divine what that honest sailor would or would not do at any given moment, more especially beneath the spur of unwonted exhilaration and joyous excitement. A thousand to one in the first flush of re-union with his betrothed, he had laid bare without a thought of harm the scheme concocted by the two in a giddy moment, and adhered to by Bertram at first on account of its plausibility and simplicity—afterwards, because he had no choice.

If Satterthwayte had told? He felt that he should know the moment the drawing-room door opened, whether Satterthwayte had told, or not.

The room seemed to spin round, and——

"Oh, Mr. Bertram, I wish I had sent the carriage for you," exclaimed Lady Margaret's voice in its most gracious accents. "I am so sorry. It could so easily have called for you when Captain Satterthwayte was fetched from the station. And you look so tired to-night;" he was pale and shaking, bewildered too by a sense of reprieve, and a desperate anxiety to turn it to account. "You must have the carriage to take you home," concluded Lady Margaret, in her kindest manner.

She thought that his lips murmured gratitude. He himself did not know what they said.

When Captain Satterthwayte came down, big, bronzed, and bearded, making the furniture rattle as he burst in, and betraying no less his surprise than his satisfaction at the sight of the guest whom Lady Margaret had risen to present, Bertram's face was a sight to see. Happily in real life such a face does not attract the attention it ought to do, and aware of this, the young man was possibly even afraid that it might not be significant enough. He clutched the other's hand, and wrung it in an agony.

Then he saw that all was so far safe, as the sailor, tenderly withdrawing his wounded member, eyed it and him alternately. The look said: "I understand. But you need not have broken my wrist, all the same."

"I did not know you two were acquainted," said Lady Margaret, taking the young clergyman's arm, and letting him lead her—as by virtue of his cloth she loved to do—to the head of her table. "We have never heard you mention Captain Satterthwayte. But then, of course," answering herself, "we may never have mentioned Captain Satterthwayte to you." Then she let the subject drop; it was not one likely to interest Mr. Bertram.

She congratulated herself, however, on the coincidence. It was quite a lucky hit her having made the addition to their party, especially when it proved that the young men had not only been schoolfellows, but had kept up a close friendship—as close a friendship as circumstances permitted—ever since; Bertram had stayed at Sir Philip Satterthwayte's —and apparently Sir Philip had a warm regard for his son's friend— there were hints about the family living which Lady Margaret could hardly comprehend.

The hints, it is true, were all on one side. Captain Satterthwayte was bubbling over with them, and with arch significance. But it did seem odd that if there were anything of that kind in prospect, no one at Garfords should ever have heard Mr. Bertram so much as mention the name of Satterthwayte. She must talk the matter over with Mary, and find out if Mary could throw any light upon it.

Mary was sitting upright as usual, immaculate in dress and demeanour as usual, but there was a soft light in her blue eye, and a smile upon her lips which was not often there. Lady Margaret was herself conscious of an expansion of the heart beneath the jolly uproar which made itself felt wherever Frank Satterthwayte was to be found. It would have been natural that Margaret also should have shared the general animation, but Margaret, strange to say, was out of spirits and paler than her wont. Margaret's mother could only suppose that her darling, like poor dear Mr. Bertram, was feeling tired; possibly a little overdone with too long a ride in the afternoon; and as she looked from one to the other, the robust dowager wondered what young people could be made of now-adays.

Still the dinner passed off cheerily, and in due time came to a close. The ladies rustled away, the door was shut behind them, and Bertram, with a new expression, turned and faced his friend.

"Good heavens! Frank, it has been a close thing! Why didn't you let me know you were coming? I have been expecting you for weeks; and then to be taken by surprise at the last!"

"Very jolly surprise," said the sailor, coolly. "Nice to meet old friends on the first day of one's return. Well, and how goes it?" dropping significance and smiling frankly. "How has it turned out? You seem quite at home here, and all that. And my respected mother-in-law-to-be beams upon you

through her eyeglasses as I hoped
and expected she would. Well, and
Margaret?   Am I to congratulate
you and Margaret?   You didn't look
quite the engaged couple to-night,
to be sure—I might say that one
wore a more hang-dog expression
than the other,—but that's a detail.
Come, out with it! Is it all right?"

"All right?" echoed Bertram, bitterly.   "Frank, if you had known
what you were doing, or if I had
known what I was doing, when you
planned and I agreed to carry out
this devilish plot——"

"Devilish! Oh, come, Bertram!"

"I say it *is* devilish. It was of
the devil's own making. He em-
ployed you to tempt me; and me
again to tempt Margaret. We
should never have thought of such a
thing for ourselves. And you,
Frank—you, who are as open as the
day, to suggest that I should play
the hypocrite——"

"All's fair in love and war, you know," said Frank, a trifle uneasily. "I—upon my word, I thought I was doing you a good turn. It seemed to me there was no chance for you, unless you crept up Lady Margaret's sleeve, and we all know her ladyship's proclivities. She adores parsons—but they must be parsons of a certain cut—at any rate, while they are on their promotion. As you had decided on becoming a parson before ever you met Margaret Whitmore, I saw no harm in your suiting yourself to the taste of Margaret's mother in the cut of your jib, and all that goes with it. Then we agreed that it would be best to begin the acquaintanceship on that level, and not refer to a certain jolly Oxford week, and a subsequent meeting at Henley, when Margaret was under other chaperonage. Her mother never cares to hear about that summer, as it is. She thought Miss Meg got out her horns too far, and had too good a time altogether. Even Mary—my beautiful Mary—shakes her elder-sisterly head over the want of starch in poor little Maggie's nature. They would have been horrified had they known *all* that went on, eh, Bertram? That moonlight night on the river—and the couple that were left behind on the island—eh? We won't talk about it. Why, what's the matter? You're not going to funk now, are you? Now, when we've brought it all so nearly to a conclusion—a glorious conclusion? You've played your part——"

"And taught her hers," said Bertram, suddenly rising and flinging himself into a fresh attitude like a man stung beyond endurance. "Do you know, Frank — it's almost incredible—but I swear to you that until I saw you here to-night, or even until I heard you speak just now, the whole black hypocrisy of this detestable proceeding never once showed itself before my eyes. Margaret and I fell in love with each other as a boy and girl will do in the course of a few days—almost within a few hours. One long summer evening, and the thing was done—"

"Very natural, I'm sure. Did it myself at your age." The bearded sailor nodded approval.

"Oh! but hear me out, and don't jest," quoth poor Bertram, writhing in the pangs of a tardy awakenment. "You are older than I, and know the world. I was your little chap at school, and you were good to me. And I would have licked the blacking off your shoes—you know I would. You've always meant to be my friend, Frank; and you meant it for the best when you cautioned me that if once a whisper of that happy time reached the ears of Margaret's mother it would never be anything but a memory—a wretched, sorrowful memory—for us both."

"True bill," said Captain Satterthwayte, complacently, "I did."

"And you suggested that we should both drop all appearance of ever having met before, when I came here to learn parish work as Mr. Fairclough's curate. That I should be introduced as a perfect stranger to Lady Margaret and her daughters, and make my way with them until—oh, Frank, why did you do it—why—why *did* you do it?" On a sudden a groan that was almost a sob burst from the young man's lips, his head fell down upon his hands, and the tremor which shook his slender frame betrayed the strength of the emotions within.

The cigar fell from between Frank Satterthwayte's fingers.

"Why did you do it?" repeated Bertram, in a fierce undertone. "You might have seen, you might

have guessed what it would lead to.
It has been a lie from beginning to
end.   We have never met, she and I
—never interchanged a word or look
—never touched each other's hand in
the presence of a third person, without acting a falsehood.   And the
worst of it is that I do not believe
either of us has realised this!   I
doubt if we have not even looked
upon it as legitimate and romantic.
It has been a pleasant pastime.
Sometimes I have felt as if the edge
of the precipice were perhaps rather
too thin, but the very danger was
exhilarating,—while as for Margaret,
the poor guileless child, she thinks it
must be right because *I* approve!
God forgive me!   Her crime lies at
my door as well as my own.''

"Come, come, this—this is all
nonsense, you know, Bertram.''
Captain Satterthwayte pulled himself together and shook off an uncomfortable sensation.   "You are

growing the least little bit absurd, don't you think? Call a trifle like this a 'crime'? Oh, come, you know," laying a remonstrating hand on the other's shoulder, "I expect my sudden appearance on the scene gave you a bit of a shake; and you thought that perhaps I, in the exuberance of this merry meeting, might have blurted out the truth to Margaret's sister."

"Would to heaven you had!"

"Would to heaven I had?" Satterthwayte stared. "And pray, why?"

"Because it would have saved me from doing so," said Bertram, slowly, "to Margaret's mother."

"Humph! That's it, is it? I suppose you know," looking at him keenly, "what the upshot of such a move would be?"

"I know. Yes. I have been knowing for the last hour. I am going now," with a move towards the door, "to do it."

For the moment it seemed as if he were to be allowed to do it. Then with a hasty step Satterthwayte was between him and the door handle.

"Look here, Jack. I don't want you to ruin yourself, and lay the blame on my shoulders! As you listened to me once—perhaps to your cost—you are bound to listen again."

"I am not bound."

"You are, and don't be a fool." He was pushed gently backwards towards the fireplace. "This is a bad business, I allow. I didn't think the thing out, when I let you in for it. But it's done, and can't be undone. You have Margaret to consider as well as yourself. The poor girl is head and ears in love, as anyone can see—anyone at least with half an eye—a thing which, begging her pardon, Margaret's lady mother does not possess; but I hold the key which will unlock her ladyship's heart. It was to put this into your hands," with slow, deliberate emphasis, "that I came down upon you so sharp to-night. I would not wait to write. And besides, I wanted to be in at the death. Do you take me?"

"No," said poor Bertram, bewildered. "But, for God's sake, Frank, don't propose any more——"

"I am not going to propose anything. It is you who are going to propose;" the jolly sailor laughed with keen enjoyment of his own quip. "You shall make two proposals before this evening is over, my dear fellow. You shall go to Lady Margaret as vicar-designate of Satterthwayte—aye, you may jump, but the old boy has given his word that he will retire in six months, and my father has given his that you shall have the living. Eh! D'ye hear that? It's true, and you may believe it; so that long physiognomy of yours may shorten again. The living of Satterthwayte is good enough for anyone to marry upon, and though our good hostess may be taken aback for a moment, I shall be astonished if between us we cannot work upon her to consent to your speaking to Meg this very night. Think of it, Bertram! By George! You shall go home an engaged man! And though it would be too much to expect that we should have both weddings on the same day, still, by the spring, when you are installed parish priest among the old folks at home, and take possession of your pretty vicarage, it could be made ready for a bride; and I might leave my wife with her sister if I have to be off to sea again. At any rate, I fancy it would weigh something with my future mother-in-law that in years to come her girls would no more be separated than in years past. The vicarage is actually within the park palings, you know,——''

"Stop," said Bertram, hoarsely. As the other spoke he had been looking from side to side with the air of a hunted animal round whom the toils were gathering fast, and twice had opened his mouth to speak, and twice had closed it again. Both hands were fast clenched. "Stop—tempter." Then with instant compunction: "No, no, Frank, I did not mean it. Forgive the word. But, Frank, you who are an honest fellow, do you know what you are doing? You have drawn a picture" —his eyes gleamed; "it would be simply *everything* to me," he murmured. "I love you and yours. I love that part of the country. I hope and trust I could do my duty among you all, and yet be myself— my own true self as you have known me in years gone by. And with Margaret for my wife——''

"You would be as happy as the day is long. All right. I thought you'd see it so. Well, now, you can't reproach me any more——"

"I said 'Stop,'" said Bertram, in a low voice. "Have you thought of the price which has to be paid for it all?"

"The—price?"

"I am to go to Margaret's mother with a lie in my hand. I, a Christian gentleman! A man who has taken upon himself to live a higher life even than that of ordinary Christians! I am to——"

"Cock-a-doodle-doo-o-o! Cut it, Jack! Don't let us in for any more of that high falutin rot. You are simply to go on as you are doing. To be as you have been for the past four or five months. Some day or other, when all is squared up between you two, Margaret may confess——"

"Margaret? Poor child! You

think I would be a coward, too, Frank?"

"Confess yourself, then, if you like the job. Only take your own time and place. When the engagement is given out and everybody has heard of it, you will have Lady Margaret at your mercy. She wouldn't dare back out. And though you might, and probably would both have a *mauvais quart d'heure*, you could look on that as the proper penance for your iniquity, if you're so keen on penance. I should wait till Mary was out of the way," added the speaker, after a pause. "It would be easier for Margaret. And if you like to depute me to break it to my girl, I think I could manage her," he concluded, with the confidence of a happy lover.

There was a long silence. Each knew that the crucial moment had arrived. "If he is obstinate now," quoth Frank Satterthwayte to himself, "Heaven have mercy on us both!" He would not try another syllable of argument; he felt he had said all he could say. And now?

Bertram's features, drawn and stiffened, repelled alike sympathy and counsel. It was plain that the fight within must be fought out by himself alone.

Only a few minutes by the clock ticking on the mantelpiece, yet to each the interval seemed an age, ere by a sudden electrical shock the eyes of both flashed into each other, and something very like an oath escaped from the lips of one. Bertram simply nodded his head, and walked from the room.

Captain Satterthwayte lit another cigar. "I shall hear him go out of the front door presently," muttered he.

.   .   .   .

How it all ended has long been a matter of history. No one beyond the initiated few ever heard the tale of that strange evening at Garfords —that evening which brought to light such surprises for all; which began with such suffering and humiliation, such storm and stress, and ended in such a heaven of peace and joy.

Bertram himself felt as if another Power than his own were at work on his behalf; as if the victory which he had gained in that dumb struggle with his baser self had expiated after some fashion of its own all that had gone before, and rendered him strong to brave the downfall of his hopes, as well as the scorn and reproaches which he too well knew would deservedly fall to his share.

He went into Lady Margaret's presence prepared for this—prepared for everything. In his heart there was but one thought, to confess his fault without an iota of reservation, and to take upon his own head the blame of it in every respect. He would not mention Frank Satterthwayte's name, and he would plead for Margaret; a stab went through his heart when he guessed how it would be when he began to plead for Margaret. He would be desired not to mention the name of Lady Margaret Whitmore's daughter. He would be accused, and rightly, of perverting her conscience and her judgment. He would have his holy profession thrown in his teeth—rightly also. He would be bidden to leave the house, and have it hinted that he would do well to withdraw from the neighbourhood also.

Would Lady Margaret insist upon Mr. Fairclough's being informed of his curate's disgraceful conduct? He felt that he would have to obey any demands and comply with any terms dictated. It all passed through Bertram's mind like a flash of revelation as he walked across the

short space between the doors of the
two rooms. But he never wavered.
One moment he stood still, his hand
upon the door handle. One quick
sigh escaped as a burst of sweet
music from within assailed his ears;
and one upward glance implored pity
and aid for a poor soul in its
extremity, and then——

"Lady Margaret," said Bertram,
walking up to a distant armchair,
"would you be good enough to grant
me a few minutes' private conversation? May we retire into the back
drawing-room?"

Looking back, he beheld the scene
with dazed and incredulous eyes.
Lady Margaret's start of surprise;
next her gracious signification of
assent; then her frozen muteness
of amazement; finally—what took
place finally he could scarce, even in
the retrospect, behold at all. Could
it have been his own voice which so
steadily proclaimed his own base-

ness? Could it have been he himself
who so unflinchingly painted its
darkest colours, and called upon his
auditor to note how black they were?
He had hidden nothing, extenuated
nothing,—and through it all a rigid,
upright figure sat and listened as
though petrified. When the end
came he waited in vain for the pent-
up outburst which must follow.

Then he realised that Lady Margaret was a woman of a finer nature
than he had given her credit for
being. She would not stoop to add
her reproaches to his own. It was
sufficient that he had abased himself; she would not heap added
humiliation upon his head. He perceived that he was to be allowed to
depart without further torture.

And he had turned to do so, and
even advanced a pace towards re-
treat, when a thin hand was put out
with a motion of arrest, and a faint,
quavering voice—curiously unlike

Lady Margaret's voice—pronounced his name. Looking round he saw, not the stately lady of the manor, the awe-inspiring mistress of Garfords, but an old, old woman, with tears running down her cheeks.

"Stay a moment, sir, until—until I am able to speak." Then the jewelled hand beckoned him to approach, and with faltering steps he obeyed. Lady Margaret was seeking for her handkerchief; seeking hither and thither in vain. Bertram, with the gesture of a son, drew an unfolded one from his pocket and reverently tendered it. As he did so, she caught him fast, as though afraid he would again essay to depart, ere she could compose her broken breath and subdue the quivering muscles of her face. He wondered what was coming—what could be coming?

And at length—marvel of marvels —a whisper the most extraordinary, the most incredible, fell upon his ear. Was it Lady Margaret speaking? Or was it a Diviner Voice which breathed through her lips the words just faintly audible: "If ye do not forgive, neither will your Father which is in heaven forgive your trespasses."

.   .   .   .   .   .

Nor from that moment, nor to the very end of her days, was the subject ever again alluded to by Bertram's mother-in-law. Where Lady Margaret forgave, she forgave freely; when she trusted, she trusted implicitly. Bertram's voluntary confession, supplemented as it was by Captain Satterthwayte's account of his own share in the affair—an account which in justice it should be said was rendered with strict truthfulness, Frank having been more impressed than he cared to own by the example of his friend—all so wrought upon a nature nobler than

the world had ever guessed it to be,
and upon a spirit genuinely influ-
enced by the great doctrines of
Christianity, that in her anxiety to
restore the penitent to himself, to
mark her appreciation of the true
worth of his character, and to show
that its solitary lapse from integrity
was to be no bar to her renewed and
even deepened esteem, Lady Margaret evinced an overflowing tenderness of generosity which amazed all
who knew her.

Bertram became her favourite son-
in-law, albeit she soon discovered
him to be by nature the merriest,
lightest-hearted fellow alive. She
secretly comforted herself for this by
the reflection that, in spite of all, he
still did undeniably possess a clerical
exterior.

ONLY KITTY

Only Kitty

A "KODAK" OF LONDON LIFE

❧❧❧

Kitty was pretty,
And Kitty was witty,
But Kitty, alack! was only Kitty.

❧❧❧

It was "only Kitty" who had
received such a very odd invitation,
that all the feminine heads of the
family were gathered together to
smile over the letter which conveyed
it. If it had been either of the two
elder Miss Masterdons who had been
invited to spend a month in Gordon
Square, Bloomsbury, during the
height of the London season, all
concerned would almost have felt as
if Maud and Ethel had been in-
sulted. Maud and Ethel were such
very grand young ladies.

But now that it was only Kitty to whom kind old Mrs. Benetfink—(the wealthy and worthy kinswoman whom no one wished to offend, but whom it was sometimes rather awkward to evade)—had extended the finger of hospitality, Mrs. Masterdon and her daughters looked at each other, as we have said, with a smile, while Kitty raised a shout of joy.

"Oh, let me go! Let me go!" cried she, prancing up and down. "Father, say I'm to go," darting up to the old squire, who, all unconscious, placidly opened the door of the room. "Father, do be on my side," seizing him by the arm and shaking it vigorously. "You know you always are on my side, aren't you? And if you say I am to go, mother won't refuse."

"Eh?" said he, stopping short, and looking from one to the other. "What?"

"Oh now, father, do promise me

before they begin. Don't listen to anyone but me. You say that I'm to go,—"

"But how *can* I say? I—upon my word—I don't know what it is all about. Do some of you explain." And the poor gentleman looked round for aid; though it is noteworthy that he did not attempt to shake off the vehement little gadfly which had fastened upon him. "What is she rushing at me like this for?" he demanded, finally.

"It is only Kitty, you know," began his eldest daughter, with the usual condescending intonation. "She always flies into a fever about everything. Kitty, don't worry father. Of course he will agree to whatever mother thinks right."

"Oh, of course!" assented he, with a touch of quiet grimness.

"And so if you will let mother think it over, and not be in such a hurry, I dare say you will get what

you want. It is an invitation from
Mrs. Benetfink, father."

"Mrs. Benetfink? Oh!"

"She wants Kitty to go to her
next Monday to spend a few weeks."

"A month," bursts in Kitty

"A few weeks or a month,"
amended the narrator. "It is really
very kind of Mrs. Benetfink, and
well meant, and all that; and, of
course, she does not know any
better."

"Know any better?" echoed
Kitty's little shrill voice.

"Oh, we all know how you feel!"
continued Miss Maud, not unkindly.
"You are wild to go anywhere and
everywhere. It's all one to you
whether it is Belgravia or Bloomsbury, Mayfair or Wapping; I believe
you would cheerfully start for .Beth-
nal Green to-morrow if anybody
would put you into the train."

"Well, well, it's only Kitty,"
quoth Mrs. Masterdon, with the

usual half indulgent, half contemptuous smile, "and she is so
young and inexperienced!"—Kitty
nodded delightedly at each adjective
—"that all neighbourhoods are alike
to her. And really it does not matter, you know, where an *un-come-out*
girl goes"—pausing for reflection.

"I think she ought to go," said
Ethel, slowly. Ethel's decisions
were final at Monk's Cary. Kitty
nearly fell at her sister's feet.

.   .   .   .   .   .

Mr. and Mrs. Masterdon, albeit
people of family and fortune, had no
town-house of their own, and were
indisposed to rent one, and undergo
all the fatigue and turmoil of the
London season during the months of
the year when their own beautiful
country-seat was most congenial to
them, and when the effort was not
absolutely necessary from other
motives than those of enjoyment.

According to their views—or, to

be strictly correct, according to Mrs. Masterdon's views—it would have been their bounden duty to make an annual move as soon as the ages of her daughters seemed to demand recognition, had she not by good hap been exempt from pressing the point in the case of her eldest, who had been engaged and married—married handsomely, too—before ever she had been presented at Court.

A few county balls and shooting dinner parties had done the business almost ere the young lady's parents themselves had opened their eyes to the fact that there was a suitor in the case; and since then there had always been Lady Latimer's house in South Street for Maud and Mabel to resort to when the month of May came round.

Letitia was well pleased to have her sisters. She was an amiable girl, perfectly well-conducted, perfectly satisfied with her own position, and benevolently ready to do what she could towards helping the younger ones to similar good fortune.

Her husband, usually called "Little Bob," was a good-natured, gossipy little fellow, with plenty of friends, nothing to do, and all day to do it in.

To the care, then, of this young couple Mrs. Masterdon was well pleased to despatch her daughters whenever they desired to exchange the woods and fields of Monk's Cary for the glitter and gloss of Rotten Row, the while she herself remained behind to attend to her flower borders, cut her lavender, and dry her rose-leaves; and on the occasion with which this little story opens, Maud and Ethel were just preparing to depart for their annual sojourn.

"I shall go up with you when I go to Mrs. Benetfink's," said Kitty, gleefully. "I shall go with you as far as the station,—but I sha'n't want

you a bit beyond. Mrs. Benetfink
is going to send her own carriage
for me, and I shall drive off in it all
by myself; and then I'm to see no
more of you all the time I'm in Gordon Square—isn't that it? You
won't come prowling after me, and
wanting to know what I'm doing,
and where I'm going?" (She did
not perceive the covert amusement
in two pairs of eyes as she spoke.)
"Because, you know, though I am
very fond of you both, I do want to
be quite on my own *hook*," pursued
she, anxiously. "I think it will be
such fun; and I think it's a splendid
idea not to tell Mrs. Benetfink anything about your being up, if we can
only keep from meeting; and London is such a very big place that I
dare say we shall be able to manage
that," she added, reflectively;
"though, of course, I shall see you
sometimes in the Park—but oh, I
say, Maud," breaking off short,

"what if Mrs. Benetfink sees you too?"

Maud took her sister's hand. "Now, Kitty, listen; and try to be a little grown-up, and reasonable, and sensible. Though you are only seventeen, you are not a child; and you can surely begin to understand things. We think it will be easiest to say nothing about our being in Town; but if Mrs. Benetfink recognizes us anywhere when she is out driving with you, all you need say is that we are staying with Letitia, and that you will write and let us know if she would like us to call. Don't do this unless you are obliged," emphatically. "You see, Mrs. Benetfink is not quite—quite——"

"Oh, I know she's rather vulgar!" said Kitty, frankly. "*I* don't mind; but I dare say Letitia would curl up sometimes. I'll take care," nodding merrily. "We vulgarians sha'n't cross the path of you grandees. We are going to enjoy ourselves in our own way; and we don't want *you*, any more than you want *us;* and if I pass you sitting aloft behind your powdered and cockaded men when I am in my humbler carriage, I shall just wink to you and grin to myself as I go by."

"For goodness' sake, don't wink, Kitty!"

"Mayn't I wink? Well, then, I shall give you a *fearfully* knowing look, and you shall see that I am laughing to myself. Or, suppose I drop my parasol between Mrs. Benetfink and you, and make a face like this," puckering up her mouth, "for your and Letitia's benefit?"

"You understand, Kitty, that it is only on Letitia's account that we— we,—of course Letitia has Bob's people to think of. In London one has to be so very particular whom

one knows. No doubt Mrs. Benetfink would like to know Letitia very
much——"

"No doubt she would do nothing
of the kind," thrust in Kitty.
"Letitia's a fine lady, and Mrs.
Benetfink is just a dear, old, rather
common one; as nice as she can be,
and not at all troubling her head
about doing the 'right thing,' and
going to the 'right places,' as you
swells do."

"Kitty, dear child, don't say 'you
swells.'"

"Why not? You *are* swells, you
and Ethel. I always think how
gorgeous you look when you set
forth all in your best, holding your
heads in the air, for some grand
party or other; and I am sure to
hear afterwards how you've been
admired and made a fuss about.
But you will never turn *me* into a
swagger Miss Masterdon. I'm only
Kitty, and I like to enjoy myself;

and though Mrs. Benetfink does
sometimes make me laugh a little
down in my throat, it's not *her* I'm
laughing at, it's only her way of
looking at things. And as for letting
her go to a house where she wasn't
wanted"—the colour rose in Kitty's
cheek—"you may be very sure I
shall take care she doesn't do *that!*"
she concluded, proudly.

"Say no more," whispered Maud
to Ethel. She perceived the right
chord had been touched.

Directly the train stopped at
Waterloo Station, Kitty was on the
alert to bid her sisters farewell, and
be off by herself with her own footman, whom her quick eyes espied in
a twinkling, and whom she had
been instructed how to distinguish
by a ribbon passed through his
buttonhole. Mrs. Benetfink had
herself tied the ribbon there, and
impressed upon Andrew, a raw
Scotch youth, good of heart but

sluggish of brain, to be as clever as he could in picking out her young lady visitor from among the train's passengers.

What Andrew's cleverness might have amounted to boots not here to inquire, for Kitty saved him the trouble of exerting it.

"There he is! That's my man!" she cried, with keen exultation; "and just where he should be—just where I was looking for him! And I dare say that's your creature, all painted and powdered, gaping up and down, and hardly taking the trouble to turn his head this way! Isn't that your creature? I knew it was! As like Letitia as he can be— I mean as like Letitia's footman—I mean—never mind, I'm off. Good-bye to you both. Bless you! bless you! I hope you'll enjoy yourselves one half as much as I mean to do. I say," turning back with a momentary hesitation, "you might just drop

me a line now and then to tell me
what you are about."

"Of course we shall write to you,
child!" said Maud, kindly. "What
an absurd girl you are! You speak
almost as if we should be ashamed of
you, and you know it is not that at
all."

"Oh, I know it is not that!" said
Kitty, cheerfully, though her eyelids quivered a little. "I know all
about it. But it just seemed rather
odd to be saying 'Good-bye' and yet
to be stopping in the same place."

But in a few minutes she had forgotten all about the oddness. Kitty had
such a sweet, frank nature, and such
perfect trustfulness in the good will
of all about her, that it only needed
an affectionate kiss from either sister, and the repeated assurance that
she would be thought of and com-
municated with (at intervals), for
her to cast off the little cloud which
had for a moment overshadowed her

spirits, and for all to be sunshine once more.

As she drove off in Mrs. Benetfink's solid, comfortable carriage, which, to her glee, was empty, her hostess having been detained at the last moment, she indulged herself by making the promised "face" as she passed Lady Latimer's elegant victoria, and neither Maud nor Ethel could resist laughing in response.

It was only Kitty—and their hearts felt rather soft towards Kitty as she rolled away.

By the time Kitty arrived in Gordon Square her happiness, importance, and pleasurable anticipation were a treat to see. The friends, whose unexpected call had detained Mrs. Benetfink in her own drawing-room, fell in love with her young visitor on the spot. They had never beheld anything prettier than Kitty's bounding rush into the old lady's arms. "And wasn't it kind of her to think of me?" she appealed to the other two, whose sympathising faces betokened appreciation and begot confidence. "And to have me all by myself! Just what I like best! To go about with *her*, you know, all day long! And no one else to interfere! No one else to be talked to! Just we two together! Won't it be delightful?"

The visitors gone, "Now let us talk," cried Kitty, settling down. "Let us plan it all out. It begins with to-morrow, doesn't it?"

"Well, I took tickets for to-night——"

For *to-night!*" screamed Kitty.

"For the Botanic Fête," nodded Mrs. Benetfink. "So now, shall we go up and see your room? My maid is putting out your things; and, Kitty," nervously, "I—I just took the liberty of getting in these——" for laid upon the bed in Kitty's room

were three lovely new made-up
skirts; one with a neat little bodice,
the other two with materials awaiting construction. "Being a relation
and an old body, and your own particular friend, I thought your mamma
would allow me," murmured Mrs.
Benetfink, trying not to look guilty. ·
"You see, it's so difficult to get
things attended to for all; and your
sisters—so I just took it on myself.
And there's a nice little dressmaker
at Marshall's," smiling across the
bed, "who is coming in to-morrow
morning, first thing after breakfast.
Well now, I *am* glad you're pleased.
I thought you would be," returning
a rapturous embrace. "And here is
Blossom to look after you and settle
you in. Blossom says if you mind
sleeping alone in this big room that
Lizzie—that's the under-girl—can
have a bed in the dressing-room
here," opening a side door. "Oh,
the bed's there already, I see! And

quite right too, Blossom. I am glad you went and did it without stopping to ask questions. So now I'll be off, and you take your time, and shake off all your dust. If you would like a warm bath, the bath-room's next door, and it might freshen you up for the evening? Blossom will get it ready, and you can pop in while she's unpacking. See to it, Blossom. And oh, Kitty! there's one thing more—these roses," turning to a bunch on the toilet-table. "Although you come from a land of roses, I dare say you won't despise them, and I like to see a young girl with a posy. Put them in your belt to-night, my dear; and you'll always have a flower to wear whenever you're going out. If I forget, just ask me for it. There now," looking round, "is that all?"

"I should think it must be all," said Kitty, looking straight at her with moist eyes, "because there really isn't anything else left to wish for."

.   .   .   .

It was one of the hottest days of the year, so that there was perhaps some excuse for people being languid and peevish, especially people who had been toiling after pleasure for many days and nights together, and who, if they had found it, were scarcely inclined to allow as much.

By their listless attitudes and disjointed conversation—if conversation it could be called—any one could have told that it was a family party which was gathered together, or, strictly speaking, which drooped in company within the shaded windows of a small house in Mayfair. One by one they had strayed in from the flowering balcony, vowing that it was hotter without than within; and now the three sisters, Letitia, Maud, and Ethel, fanned themselves with their pocket-handkerchiefs, or hung their arms by their sides, as they endeavoured by absolute rest from every sort of exertion to prepare for the moment when effort must again be made.

Yet no one suggested the idea of abandoning the effort. Of course they would go to the Embassy Ball; and of course it would be like every other ball, crowded and gorgeous, and unsatisfactory; and they would come away fatigued to death, and fit only to drop on to their pillows, and remain there till to-morrow's sun should be high in the heavens, making fresh demands, which were yet the demands of all its predecessors.

"This London season is really very hard work," observed Letitia, at last, as sapiently as though the remark had never been made before. "I am sure I don't know how one ever lives through it. If one could pick and choose—but that's just what one can't do. People talk about going out 'a little.' But who ever does go out 'a little'? You are either *in it*, or you are *out of it*—at least that's what I find."

"It is certainly better to be 'in it' than 'out of it.'" This was Ethel's wisdom.

"Of course one could enjoy it more if it could be taken by inches," subjoined Maud; "for instance, if one could turn weeks into months ——"

"Oh, I don't know that I want months of this!" interposed Lady Latimer, hastily, missing the point. "I am always thankful when the season is over, and the order is given to pack up and be off. I really think"—but what she really thought was never destined to be known.

The door opened.

"Ha, I thought I'd find you all melting away in here," quoth Sir Robert, poking in a little brisk face. "Here's Syd saying the weather's glorious," indicating a handsome sunburnt edition of himself. "Syd likes the heat," continued little Bob, dropping into a chair. "He says it makes him feel more fit than he has done since he came home from the East."

"I should not mind the heat if I could take things as easily as Captain Latimer does," said Maud Masterdon, throwing a half-reproachful glance at Sir Robert's brother. "If one could make up one's mind to go nowhere, live at a club—"

"That's what he does—lives at his club," dashed in her brother-in-law. "He is to be found standing about in that nice cool hall, morning, noon, and night. I'm hanged if he isn't in the right of it too. It's beastly being on the rush all the time; only—I say, doesn't it get a bit monotonous, Syd?"

"It does, rather," said Syd, cheerfully.

"Then why not come with us
sometimes, Sydney?" Here was a
chance for which Letitia had been
longing. "You know how often we
have asked you."

"I know you're awfully good,"
said he.

"But you won't come, all the
same."

Then little Bob laughed aloud.
"You won't catch him, not you. Do
you suppose it hasn't been tried
before? He never answers his invitations. I believe it's too much
trouble even to tear them up; they
are just left to accumulate."

"Oh, he's simply too fine for anything!" Letitia tossed her head a
little, whilst her sisters maintained
the silence of discreet young women
who feel their charms unappreciated.

"I come to *your* parties, you know,
Letitia——" began Captain Latimer.

"When?" shot like a cannon-ball
from Letitia's lips.

"To be sure, I did not come, but I meant to, last week——"

"And you refused my dinner invitation for next."

"That's it!   At him, Letitia!" Sir Robert rubbed his hands in glee. "He's too big a swell altogether. He always was too grand for me; and I believe he never would come near the house, if I didn't go myself and hook him right out of that old club door." As he spoke he made an affectionate grimace which betokened a perfect understanding between the brothers. "He only came now because he wants to know if I may go with him to-night," concluded the speaker.

"To-night?   Go with him to-night?" Letitia sat bolt upright in an instant.   Her husband go with his brother, instead of his brother going with them all!   And she would have been so particularly pleased to take Captain Sydney Lati-

mer to the Embassy Ball, for which
he had his own invitation, and
where, if he did not know more
people than she herself did, he would
be welcomed by some of high importance, and would be intimate
with several to whom an introduction might be useful. She was now
really vexed as well as alarmed.

"Bob told me he was going with
you to a ball," said Captain Latimer, patting on the head a little dog
which had run up to him. "Balls
aren't much sport, at least to a man
who doesn't dance. I am going to a
play—no, I believe it ought not to
be called a play; it's an 'Entertainment,' that's the dodge; but all the
same, I hear it is awfully funny, and
I want to see Corney Grain in it. I
hear he is awfully good in his new
piece——"

"Corney Grain!" exclaimed three
pairs of lips at once. "Why, that is
at the German Reeds!" appended

Lady Latimer, almost in a whisper. Then she turned upon her husband such a face of blank consternation as made him leap into the air and wring his hands in ecstasy.

` "It *is* the German Reeds, by Jove!" he cried. "The murder's out, by Jove! I thought it would nearly kill 'em!" to his brother. Then to his wife: "He won't go near your Embassy Ball. He won't go to any of the first parties in London. He can hardly be got even for a dinner, and even by his best friends,— and here he has set his heart on going to laugh at the most squalid show in the whole place, and wants me to go with him; and, by Jove! I am going too!"

The ladies sat absolutely mute.

"I'll do my level best to bring him on to the ball afterwards," proceeded little Bob, anxiously.

"We ought to be much honoured," replied his wife, dropping her eyelids.

But the shot told. She made no further opposition; and Sir Robert, saying he would not be ten minutes dressing, flew upstairs three steps at a time; while Captain Latimer explained that it had been arranged that the two were to dine together at his much-reviled club, in order that the early hour at which the "squalid show" commenced might not inconvenience the Mayfair household.

As it was, the two arrived late at the entertainment for which they were bound; and the piece was in full swing as they took their seats in the somewhat dingy hall, full in every part, and proportionately warm. The audience was not a smart one, and Kitty Masterdon had her eye in a moment on the two figures who seated themselves in the vacant places on the other side of the aisle, within a few feet of where she and Mrs. Benetfink were enjoying them-

selves to their hearts' content.
"Two swells," said Kitty to herself,
—then the next moment: "Oh, I
say, one is Bob!" She could not
have been more surprised if Bob had
walked into the drawing-room in
Gordon Square.

"That is Bob," she repeated,
watching the two with interested
eyes, "and that other thing's his
brother that Letitia thinks so much
of. ·Well, now, this is a joke! They
will never see me—the brother
would never know me if he did—
and I shall tell Maud and Ethel
afterwards that my places cannot be
so vulgar after all, when this grand
Captain Latimer thinks them worth
coming to;" and she chuckled with
renewed delight. "He looks quite
festive," she proceeded, presently,
"and there is Bob laughing like anything! Whenever there is anything
very good, we shall all laugh together, and nobody be any the

wiser!'' She then gave herself up to the play.

"There's a little girl over there enjoying herself hugely," thought Captain Latimer, and he could not resist looking round once or twice when an infectious trill of merriment from the other side of the aisle broke upon his ear. Kitty had a charming laugh.

Kitty had on her new rose-coloured dress, which matched exactly the bright tint in her cheeks, and enhanced the blue of her limpid eyes and the gold of her overflowing hair. She looked what she was—a lovely, happy young girl, without a care in the world, without a thought which could not be laid bare to every eye.

So radiant, so animated, so full of sparkling life and vivacity did she seem, that it was hardly to be wondered at if even amongst a crowd of other youthful faces hers seemed to stand out pre-eminently, especially when viewed in conjunction with the benevolent glances of a silvery-haired old lady who obviously regarded her charge with more than favour. At length it came to this, that there was quite a little ring formed as it were involuntarily, of which Kitty was the centre, who all looked to her, and laughed and applauded whenever anything specially droll on the stage made them sure of the joyous response it would call forth.

"By Jove! she has the jolliest little laugh I ever heard!" And Captain Latimer began quite to listen for the laugh.

But he did not tell Bob about it; and Bob, who was entirely occupied with what was going forward, drinking it all in as though the wit were the most wonderful and the comedy the most absorbing to which he had ever hearkened, missed the by-play.

"Bob's all right," Kitty told herself. "Good little Bob; he will
never see me across that big brother
of his. Sydney must be nearly a
foot taller, and he's ever so much
better-looking. What fun it is! We
must get away as quick as we can
when it is over, though, or I should
never hear the last of it from the
girls." (Kitty was wont to desig-
nate her august sisters as "the girls"
in internal colloquy, her reverence
for them and their opinions being
only skin-deep.)

She rather surprised Mrs. Benetfink now by the precipitation with
which she sprang to her feet almost
before the curtain fell, and the
urgency with which she caught up
her own wrap, and whirled the old
lady's round her shoulders.

"There's no hurry, my dear;" but
Kitty could not be made to understand that there was no hurry. She
was halfway down the aisle before

her good-humoured chaperon was well out of her chair, and in her heart was saying: "She can catch me up outside; I sha'n't go beyond the hall. I can sneak behind the people there, and watch my two swells go by; then I can pounce on Mrs. Benetfink, and we'll toddle merrily home together."

But there was destined to be a hitch in the programme. Within the next few minutes there was a disturbance in the outer hall which somewhat blocked the exit of those within.

"What a jolly long time it takes to empty this place!" exclaimed Captain Latimer to his brother, as the two leisurely strolled down, staring about them, and passing here and there a comment. "Rum place, isn't it? Looks a bit dusty. One would think it paid well enough to be kept in better repair. And they might open a few more doors, and not keep us all night getting out."

"They are saying somebody's met with an accident outside," replied his brother. "Some woman has fallen down, and hurt herself. Hallo! Who's here?" as the figure of a young girl, by this time quite familiar to Captain Latimer, pressed its way back through the out-streaming current, and to the latter's amazement the voice which he had heard rippling so merrily throughout the evening, now in piteous accents accosted his brother, and that by the familiar appellation of "Bob."

'Why, Kitty!" exclaimed Bob. "Why—what on earth?—I did not know you were in town! It is my sister-in-law," in explanation aside. "Kitty, this is my brother Sydney—"

"Oh, yes!" Kitty disposed of the introduction with a nod, having no time to think about it. "Oh, Bob, do come!" seizing him by the hand.

"Come quickly and help me; I don't know what to do. Mrs. Benetfink has fallen and hurt her ankle—she was hurrying after me—there was such a crowd, she didn't see the step, and now I can't find the footman, and—and I don't know what to do——" almost crying.

"All right—all right," said Bob, soothingly; "you tell Mrs. Benetfink who I am, and I will take care of her; and Syd will find the footman. Is that the old lady?" in a lower tone, as they came up with a little sympathising group of which the hapless Mrs. Benetfink was the object. "Sorry to hear you have had a fall, ma'am. Pray let me see you to your carriage." In a moment Sir Robert Latimer stared away all intruders and took possession of the situation; and presently —but we really have no time to tell how it all happened—Kitty found herself seated opposite the poor old lady, her momentary trouble over, but with, alas! a black outlook for the future. Her kind friend was in great pain, and there was no doubt that the fall had been a serious one. A doctor must instantly be summoned.

"You must let me see you home," said Sir Robert, seating himself by Kitty's side. "And Syd will go for the doctor if you will tell him where."

"No, indeed, there's Andrew," gasped Andrew's mistress, struggling with herself. "Andrew knows —where—to go;" her eyes closing, as she could with difficulty articulate the last words.

"Go at once then," supplemented Sir Robert, turning to the said Andrew. "You know the doctor's house. Bring him back with you then; bring somebody, anyway. Don't you be alarmed, Kitty," turning to her; "I'm here to stand by

you, and I will see you through.   I
say, what is Syd doing?" turning
round to look.

Captain Latimer was mounting
the box seat, the footman having
already hailed a hansom, in which he
was driving off.

"Well, that's cool," murmured
Bob.   Then in a lower aside: "But,
I suppose, she won't mind," nodding
opposite.   "We will just come to the
house, and help you to get her out.
It is all right, Kitty," he added,
after a pause, for he saw that Kitty
could hardly speak.

Although Mrs. Benetfink remained
to all appearance almost insensible
to the night's proceedings, she was
wont to recur to them afterwards in
a manner that showed she was by
no means so oblivious as was supposed.

"I could not speak," she would
aver, "and I was very bad, but I
was not *so* bad as to be quite knocked

stupid. I knew well enough that I
had two fine young men to look after
me, and to help me up my own
steps, and even to my own room—
with Joseph's assisting, of course;
and as for that husband of Letitia's
I declare I could have kissed his
honest face, he looked so much concerned, and as if he could have cried
too whenever I cried out. And
there he sat with me, hand in hand,
till the doctor came, insisting upon
it that Kitty was too young, and that
she had much better be out of the
room till I was more myself. And I
do think a dearer man there never
lived. And what Kitty would do
now without him, I don't know."

The latter remark had reference to
the black outlook which, it has been
hinted, loomed before the hapless
Kitty's vision directly her immediate
anxieties were over, and the nature
of the accident ascertained.

"Yes, I am afraid it's all up with

you, Kitty." Sir Robert shook his
head after hearing the doctor's ver-
dict. "No more larks going in this
house. Now, I tell you what you
will do. You will come straight off
to us to-morrow. Letitia shall fetch
you——"

Kitty's eyes opened, and her lips
parted.

"That will make it all right, won't
it?" said Bob, kindly. And he proceeded to dilate.

"Stop," said Kitty, suddenly.
"Don't ask me; don't say another
word; it's awfully kind of you, and
you know how I should like it—but
it would look—oh, you know what it
would look like! She's the dearest
and the kindest—and to have me go
and leave her the moment she can't
take me about to things, as if I cared
for nothing else——" she broke off
with a little sob. "Don't you think
anything more about me, Bob. I
shall be quite happy here. I am

going to show Mrs. Benetfink that I love her *for herself*—and——"

"And I tell you what it is," said Bob, suddenly stepping forward, and seizing her hand in both of his. "You're a thundering good little girl —that's what you are; and I sha'n't say another word to tempt you away. You're quite right not to desert the old lady. Upon my word, I am proud of you. And I tell you what, Kitty; I will come every single day, and take you to every single place that Mrs. Benetfink had promised you"—(for confidences had passed by this time); "she won't mind my doing that, will she?"

"Oh, no!" Kitty was joyfully sure that, so far from minding, nothing would please Mrs. Benetfink better.

"Well, then, I'll come," said Bob; "and I can come in and see her and tell her the news, and Letitia shall

call. Why she hasn't called already
I'm sure I don't know. I don't
understand these things. But now,
where shall we go to-morrow?"

"We *were* going," said Kitty,
glancing at him, "to the Crystal
Palace."

"The Crystal Palace!" cried Sir
Robert, "the very thing! I haven't
been to the Crystal Palace since I
was in petticoats. What time were
you going?"

"We *had* been going," said Kitty,
with the same dubious emphasis,
"about three o'clock. We were to
drive down and have tea, and then
go to things; and have dinner, and
go to things again; and drive back
after the fireworks. To-morrow is a
firework night, and poor Mrs. Benetfink and I did want so dreadfully
to go!"

"I am sorry for Mrs. Benetfink,"
said Bob, pleasantly; "but anyhow,
you and I will go and enjoy our-

selves.   May I borrow your phaeton,
Syd?"

"I want it for myself," said Syd,
"if this young lady will give me the
pleasure of driving her."

And now began the most wonderful period of Kitty's life. She had
been so happy before, so content
with all the simple pleasures provided for her, so grateful for all the
loving kindness lavished upon her,
that it might have seemed as though
there were hardly any room left in
her heart for further emotions of a
like nature. But somehow it *was* a
different thing to dash off from her
own door in an elegant park phaeton,
behind a pair of high-stepping
horses, who never seemed to need
more than an infinitesimal share of
their master's attention, from rolling
solemnly away within a large landau
with only an old lady, however
cheerful and amiable, as her companion on the jaunt. It *was* a new

and exhilarating experience to be escorted hither and thither by two smart men, who were yet not "smart" in any way that would have lessened them in her estimation, or detracted from her comfort.

Letitia thought that as it was "only Kitty," she need not put herself out to combat Sir Robert's whim of making up to his young sister-in-law for the loss she had sustained. If Kitty liked to go with Bob, and Bob chose to take her, and Sydney Latimer chose to be of the party, there was really no harm in it. Kitty did not require to be chaperoned as yet, and though, as it was "only Kitty," it hardly mattered that she had been unearthed in her present "impossible" quarters, whose very impossibility roused Captain Latimer's compassion, still the very fact of its being "only Kitty" made it too certain that the feeling was compassion—nothing more.

This was Letitia's view of the case.

But Letitia did not know everything. She did not know, for instance, that the leafy garden within the quaint old square was a pleasant place to sit in on a summer afternoon, and that a cheery little party often camped out there for hours together, of whom one would be an old lady in an invalid chair, one a fair girl in the first flush of youth, and another a tawny-visaged soldier, whose mission it seemed to be to entertain and interest them both. Sometimes the whole afternoon would pass away thus.

On other occasions the trio would await the arrival of a fourth, preparatory to one of the excursions promised by Sir Robert, which he now showed an unexpected and most ingenious fertility in devising. Late though Bob would always be, no one would ever express the slightest

impatience at his unpunctuality.
Captain Latimer's phaeton would
crawl round and round the square,
or draw up beneath the rustling
shade of overhanging boughs, until
horses and men alike grew drowsy
'twixt heat and inactivity,—but Syd
himself was having a good time on
the other side of the railings.

He always came first, and came
by himself; he had invariably some
good reason to give for doing so.
His brother had so many engagements, whereas he had none. Bob
was "rushed" from morning to night
in the season; for his part, he liked
to take things easy. It was so jolly
sitting still, and it would be cooler
driving by-and-by when the sun had
begun to go down a little. As for
his horses, they were better standing
out under the trees than in their own
stuffy stable. He hoped Mrs.
Benetfink did not think him a nuisance for coming before the time,

but it was really so—so jolly sitting there. Evidently there was no other excuse to offer.

Of all this, Letitia, as we say, knew nothing. Neither did any of them know that when chirpy little Sir Robert perched himself on the back seat of the phaeton and smoked cigar upon cigar as he was trotted down to Kew, or Richmond, or Kingston Hill—anywhere and everywhere that Kitty had a mind to go —he was saying to himself that playing gooseberry was by no means such bad fun as people made out. Kitty was "only a child," was she? All right. Sydney was "never thinking of her," was he not? All right. It was satisfactory to have those beliefs prevail in his own home; they kept everything smooth there, while permitting him a free hand.

And he meant to have a free hand whether permitted or not. "Syd is a queer fellow," he nodded to himself, "and you have got to go his way, not expect him to go yours. Letitia wanted him for one of her sisters," with a grin; "but, by Jove! she will nearly have a fit when, after going through half the women she knows, she learns that it is only Kitty!"

Accordingly little Bob kept his secret close, and permitted not the faintest suspicion of it to leak out. Indeed, at this juncture he exhibited a cleverness unknown before; and Letitia, as well as her sisters, grew to think that there was something almost babyish in Kitty's silly demands upon her too good-natured brother-in-law.

"I really should not give in to her as you do," Lady Latimer would exclaim now and again; "you quite spoil that child."

Maud and Ethel had proposed Kitty's returning home, but Bob

stoutly combated the idea; and certainly when Kitty came to South Street there was no shadow upon her bright face, and nothing to indicate that all was not going well with her in spite of the misadventure of her hostess.

Every one in South Street was too busy to see much of Kitty—which was perhaps as well, all things considered—but Bob gravely assured them he was doing the best he could for her, and happily no one ever inquired minutely into what that "best" was. "They think that Syd still stands all day long in the hall of that old club," chuckled Sir Robert to himself, "and I don't see that it's my business to peach. Of course I could not take a full-blown young lady about like this; but Letitia says herself it is 'only Kitty,' and I suppose I am about equal to managing Kitty's affairs. They shall not be botched by interference anyway."

Never in his life had he enjoyed himself so much. He and Sydney took Kitty up the river, and gave her tea in the gardens of the old-fashioned inn beneath the Clieveden Woods, Sir Robert going off for a stroll by himself before the party took to the water again. He escorted her over Hampton Court, and was not at all surprised to find that she and Syd missed him from among the sightseers in the great tapestry hall, and went to look for him down by the water-lily pond. He piloted his inquisitive young sister-in-law down to Gravesend to lunch on board an ocean "liner," and thought the expedition quite one to suit Syd; indeed, considered it the most natural thing imaginable that his brother should find the vessel and its equipment so interesting, and such a novelty (although Captain Latimer had sailed to every quarter of the globe), that he must needs follow Kitty up and down and round and round, from the captain's cabin to the engineer's gangway. "I am about running dry now," he told himself, however, at the close of this last excursion. "By Jove! I can't think of much more," shaking his head wisely.

He took his brother into confidence as they trotted home from Gordon Square in a hansom.

"I think I have done pretty well for you, Syd. Don't you think that now—hum—ah——?"

"Yes, I do think that now—hum —ah —"; retorted Syd, frankly. "To-morrow is Sunday, you know. You need not come along this way on Sunday," pointing backwards with his thumb, "but I will look you up in the evening. Shall you be in about—say eight o'clock?"

About eight o'clock Sir Robert was pacing his front drawing-room restlessly to and fro, and absolutely refusing to go in to dinner, alleging that Sunday evening dinner could surely wait five minutes when a man was expecting his brother, and when no one was particularly hungry for it.

"You are generally hungry enough," said Letitia.

"Well, I am not to-night," said Bob.

The next moment he had his head out of the window, and, with a cry that was almost a whoop of exultation, dashed down the staircase before the door-bell rang.

"There is Syd, and—and—a lady with him!" he flung back as he disappeared through the doorway.

"A lady? Who can it be?" Letitia looked round at the other two. "Bob seems quite excited. What a noise he is making in the hall! Is he going to bring them up? Or shall we go down, and take them into the dining-room? What can be the meaning of all that noise?" as

voices and laughter in joyous confusion grew more and more distinctly
audible above stairs, the door having
been left ajar by Sir Robert in his
flight.

"They are coming up, I think,"
said Maud, listening; and she and
Ethel glanced at each other. They
thought they were prepared for what
was to follow, and guessed what
would be expected of them when
Captain Sydney Latimer should be
ushered in, and present the lady
whose arrival had caused such a
commotion. They were ready with
the best smiles they could muster,
when a swift patter of steps was
heard upon the staircase, and were
almost disappointed when the light
form which darted in, all smiles,
tears, and incoherence — all em-
braces, excuses, and extravagances—
proved to be that of—only Kitty!

Had Kitty gone crazed? What
was there to kiss, and hug, and cry

about? What had happened? What was—what could be—the meaning of it all?

If it had been any one else! But—— "But, by Jove! I thought it would make you sit up!" cried little Bob, almost beside himself with excitement. "I knew how you'd feel! It is 'only Kitty,' is it? Ask this fellow here," pushing Captain Latimer forward, "what he has to say to that. *He* doesn't say 'only Kitty,' I can tell you. He—oh, I say, Letitia," all in a moment the speaker's face changed, his eyelids fell, a contrite seriousness overspread his whole countenance, "I am so sorry I kept dinner waiting for only Kitty," he sighed, penitently.

A TERRIBLE MOMENT

A Terrible Moment

❧❧❧

"Great floods have flown from simple
sources."
—*All's Well that Ends Well.*

❧❧❧

Lina sat frowning over her house-
books. Who does not frown over
house-books? Who does not know
the look of the hateful little pile,
always neatly adjusted, with the
red-glazed, gilt-lettered one — the
bête noire of the whole collection—
the butcher's book, lying blatantly
on the top? Why is it always in the
front, leading, as it were, its
minions in the rear? Let house-
keepers say.

Poor little Caroline Lambert was
not much of a housekeeper; indeed,
nature never designed her for a

housekeeper at all. But when her
mother died, and Lina had been
taken into confidence about the family affairs—that is, had been openly
confided in, for from earliest childhood she had silently understood
many things which had sobered gay
insouciance—she had taken a great
resolve: she was going to fight the
world as her poor, brave, gentle parent had done, and be the real, though
unacknowledged head of her father's
house.

The world with her—the world
which had to be fought and con-
quered—resolved itself mainly into
the detestable above-mentioned
house-books; they lay at the root of
the thoughtful brow, the too-serious
eye, and the somewhat sad expression of a little mouth which seemed
as though it had been formed only
to smile or pout.

Lina was a very pretty girl, and
knew it—knew also that it was not

only the bereavement she had sustained which debarred her from the triumphs and enjoyments of fair girlhood. She had learnt even before the days of mourning that many an invitation had to be refused, and many a brilliant scene foregone which would have cost money; and that although she lived in a fairly good house, and what would have been called comfortable circumstances, there was always an underlying current running dead against her and hers, which had to be stemmed as she and they might.

For prudence' sake appearances had to be maintained; Mr. Lambert argued that nothing would have a more fatal effect on his professional career, nothing make clients more shy of putting their affairs into his hands than the fact of his having to move into a cheaper residence in a humbler part of London. He must preserve a decent exterior; he must affect to be doing well; now and again he must entertain. It was a cruel necessity, but the tide would turn some day; and if they could but manage to keep their heads above water for the present, a time would come when they should swim easily upon the surface.

"But, oh! it is so long in coming," sighed his young daughter to herself on the grim November afternoon, when she sat down to her weekly task with the house-books on her lap.

She had just finished, and finished with a sigh, and was sitting looking before her with the dull dejection of spirit the occupation seldom failed to produce, when the door burst open, and swift as thought the little heap was thrown into a work-basket by her side, and concealed beneath an embroidered coverlet. She would not vex her father by the sight.

It was not, however, Mr. Lambert who had returned before his time; it

was two little rosy, chubby, merry
creatures who precipitated themselves on to their sister's vacant lap
without dreaming that it had been
previously occupied by intruders less
welcome than themselves.

"Are you alone? We thought you
would be alone," cried little Gladys,
bustling up; "and nurse said we
might come if there was nobody
here."

"Nurse only said we were to come
if you *wanted* us," corrected the
elder, (she was only seven, while
Gladys was but four); "but we
thought you would be sure to want
us, if there were no nasty people
here." And she mounted on
Lina's other knee with the confidence of proprietorship. The elder
sister put an arm round each.

"And we do so want to tell you
what we have been talking about,"
the little one struck in again; "it
was about shoes. Nurse says we

really *must* have shoes;" sitting
upright in order to be still more
impressive and important. "She
says we really *must;* because, you
see, the Christmas parties will be
coming on, and our old shoes will
hardly hold together," unbuttoning
with eager satisfaction a little squat
strap-shoe, and looking at it fondly,
as though its state of dilapidation
were creditable and endearing.

"Mine are as bad, and they have
been patched over and over again,"
said Florence, taking her sister's face
between her hands to make sure of
attention and sympathy. "Nurse
says the shoemaker won't undertake
to do them any more. He says it's
no use wasting more work upon
them, for they're not worth it.
That's what he says; and nurse says
she can't mend them herself, for
there's just one thing she can't manage, and that is boots and shoes.
She can make everything else."

"And she is going to make us the most beautiful frocks out of mother's old white petticoat." Gladys caressed her shoe, her blue eyes beaming.

"Oh, hush!" Florence looked shocked, and glanced apprehensively at her sister. "Nurse wouldn't like you to speak like that, Gladdie," remonstrated she, shaking her severe head. "It's only that Gladdie's so little, you know," she added, feeling all the weight of her maturer years. "*I* knew whose petticoat it was, because it came out of the big wardrobe drawer, and *I* never said anything." Then she turned her face round again: "But Gladdie *would* know what it was, and what nurse was going to do with it."

"And they will be beautiful frocks —oh! beautiful." The little one stroked her sister's hair and peered into her eyes, holding up the eyelids with her tiny fingers to make sure that all was right. "Nurse is to get some more of the holey work."

"Only a *very* little more," said Florence, anxiously. "Only just enough to go round the neck and sleeves."

"And white ribbons to tie up the arms," struck in Gladys, with rapture.

"You won't mind, will you, dear?" whispered a soft little voice on her sister's shoulder; while Florence laid down her head contentedly, and shook back her fleece of shining hair.

All the time Lina never said a word; she could not find it in her heart to check the innocent outpourings, and she knew that the faithful creature who provided for her darlings' wants and necessities would not spend a penny which could be saved; but white "party" frocks, and new morocco shoes, pointed to Christmas dissipations, in which she foresaw the one black word, "expense"; and although her little Florrie and Gladdie should not be grudged any pleasures she could give them, she looked somewhat ruefully at the little, patched shoe, which the latter still dangled by the button with a triumphant air, and thought—for she was but a girl herself—that she needed to be fitted out as much as the little ones, and had no chance of, supplying her wants as she could theirs.

Presently she drew them on to talk of other things, though this was not easy, for their imaginations had been dazzled, and the thought of the cutting and shaping going on overhead drew their thoughts like a magnet from any other topic presented to them. Lina knew by the absent-mindedness which made Florence unable to think of any appropriate adjective wherewith to "Love

her Love" in the time-honoured
nursery game, and little Gladys out
of countenance to find it was her
turn so soon again, that the thoughts
of both were roving; and although
she tried various other distractions
equally in favour with the little
couple, she was half-amused, half-
vexed, to be asked over and over
again what o'clock it was, and finally
to have it suggested that nurse
would be glad to have them go
upstairs earlier than usual in order
to set her free for the all-important
business of the frocks.

"She has got so much to do;"
Gladys jumped off her sister's knee
at last. "If she can, she is going to
contrive us some little white slips
too—that is, if you will let her have
the things. She is going to——"

"But she wants to talk to Lina
about that herself,"—Florence con-
scientiously averted every premature
disclosure,—"so we won't tease poor

Lina to-night," hugging and kissing fondly; and with "Good-night,
darling, good-night," from each
rosebud mouth, the two sprang
away into the darkness of the large,
gloomy room, and, scarce waiting to
close the door in their excitement,
tore upstairs with echoing childish
mirth, which lasted until their own
upper regions were regained, and
the intervention of the nursery door
made further sounds inaudible.
Lina looked after them with a
smileless face.

That afternoon in Regent Street
she had seen a ball-dress which another girl was buying. The other
girl was not sure whether she
wanted it or not. When the shop-
woman's back was turned, she consulted with her chaperon, (obviously
a guardian, or relation, whose mission it was to advise, but certainly
not to control), enumerating the
dresses she already possessed—the

white satin and tulle, the cream satin
and spotted net, the flowered silk
—and next inquired, would she have
any real use for more in the immediate future; and, if not, would it
not be a pity to be encumbered with
a stale robe, after a newer fashion
had set in?   Poor Lina had listened
involuntarily to it all.

She would not have minded about
a newer fashion, nor called a three-
months-old costume out of date.   A
trifling commission had been made
her excuse for strolling round the
gay department,   and   she   had
watched the scene wistfully from
behind a voluminously draped lay
figure.   A vague, foolish curiosity to
know how it would end detained her
there.   Not that she doubted for a
moment, not even from the outset.
She told herself with a faint, irrepressible bitterness, that there did
not exist a girl—a girl young and
pretty   like   herself—who   would

voluntarily refrain from the acquisition of that shining, shimmering vision of loveliness, when it came to the point.

"And really, I think you are right." The portly dowager nodded approbation when the purchase was made. "You will never see anything to suit your taste better; and with so many gay visits before you, you are sure to find it come in handy sometime."

Gay visits! Again Caroline Lambert breathed a soft, hopeless note of longing. She had no visits, gay or otherwise, before her; her acquaintance was not large, and was mainly composed of people who, although they might have agreeable engagements for themselves during the forthcoming festal season, were not in a position to be entertainers. She might be invited to a few dull dinners with her father, or perhaps to accompany her little sisters to

a children's party; but Lina was
nineteen, and craved for something
which was not precisely met by
either prospect. The vision called
up by the elder lady's prudent
exultation was inexpressibly tanta-
lising. Caroline knew what *her*
Christmas would bring. Not many
bills, perhaps; for she had steadily
kept these down, refusing to make a
purchase which could not be paid
for then and there, and by this resolution denying herself more than
any one ever knew, for the household money had to be given account
of to no one; but if Christmas-time
brought not the duns of trades-
people, it would resolve itself, never-
theless, into a tame, commonplace
affair in Mr. Lambert's household;
and his young daughter knew that
the holiday period, wont to lavish so
much on others of her age, such
thrilling possibilities, such unmeas-
ured, unexplored delights, meant to

her only a flickering ray of mild domestic sunshine, all very well in its way, but lacking something, I need hardly tell my youthful readers what.

One may be an affectionate daughter and sister, but it does not fill up the measure of one's content to have a whole merry-making season go by in making happy the hearts of two little cherubs already happy enough, or interchanging pleasantries with an easy, kindly, elderly parent, with whom, but for the tie of blood, one has nothing in common. Mr. Lambert often provoked his daughter—not consciously, for he would not have hurt the feelings of a fly—but their two natures were intrinsically and diametrically opposed; and whilst the seriousness of her demeanour and over-anxieties about what he called trifles would occasionally be felt by him as a damper to cheerfulness and a hindrance to hopeful effort, she did scant justice to the elasticity of his amiable, if somewhat volatile, dispo-sition. Each meant well, and both had a part to play in family life.

Caroline's part was the hardest, or she thought so.

"Lina? Sitting alone? Where are the children?" Mr. Lambert's voice, a blithe, lively voice, sounded in the doorway. "I expected to have found the children here," con-tinued he, producing a brown paper parcel. "I have brought them each a toy."

"Oh, papa!"

"Only a penny toy, my dear. Of one of the men in the streets. But I know it will please the little folks; I was quite taken with it myself; most amusing and ingenious. Let me show you how it goes along the carpet"—suiting the action to the words. "There now! Ha, ha, ha! Is it not comical? Can't imagine

how these things are made for the
money. Shall we have the children
down again, eh? I dare say they
are not undressed yet."

"Better keep the toys for their
Christmas presents." Caroline eyed
with reproachful disdain two little
painted men with carts racing over
the floor. "I did not mean for
their *only* presents," she made haste
to add, for her own heart responded
to the quick glance of her father's
eye. "But we *can* only give them
such very little things——"

"Surely I am not reduced to giving my own children penny toys for
their Christmas presents," said he,
pained by her tone. "I know how
good and economical you are, my
dear child; but there is such a thing
as going too far."

And Lina felt there was. She
had been absurd, exaggerating her
own envious longings, her own sense
of mortification and deprivation, to a

pitch that made the sight of her father, engrossed and amused, forgetful alike of home cares and business worries, rouse indignation, and cause her to overstep the bounds of common-sense, and mistake poverty for destitution.

The shade which passed across her father's brow restored her to herself.

"Papa, I am silly. Don't listen to me. I always have a bad hour or two after going through those wretched accounts."

"They are not worse than usual, are they, my dear?"

"Not at all worse, rather better; only——" She paused, and then the truth burst out. "Only, papa, we never get any *good* of it all; we pay and pay, and it takes every farthing we possess just to *live*—to keep a roof over our heads, and have food on the table, and clothes to wear. And they are only common, necessary clothes—only clothes we cannot possibly do without. I hardly dare look in at a shop window——"

Mr. Lambert looked scared; he was easily scared.

"Is it as bad as that, my poor child? You have not proper clothes?"

"Oh, I did not say *proper* clothes; I have a hat, and a jacket, and a frock. I have even two frocks, wonderful to relate, and a shabby old dinner-dress."

"In which you always look remarkably pretty. For all their finery, I never see that other girls cut you out."

Alas! Something of the same thought had been playing the mischief in poor little Lina's bosom all the afternoon. She knew she could have shone, held her head with as high an air, danced with as light a step, and prattled with as musical a voice, as any one in the gay assemblages of which as yet she had only beheld reflections—reflections which did but invest her with desire for the unattainable: how unattainable she alone seemed to realise.

"Papa, I try"—a little struggle with herself—"I try not to be discontented; but it is so hard to have to put *everything* aside—even the chances that do come now and then —because we cannot afford to go about like other people——"   .

"Of course, my dear, it is a deprivation; I feel it so myself."

"But not as I do," cried she, breathing quickly.   "You have seen, and known, and lived; but I— the world is beyond me—I long to feel it, and touch it, and I can't. Whichever way I turn we are so hemmed in by poverty."

"Just so.   'Hemmed in,'" assented he, with approbation.

"Poverty that no one sees or recognises; that you yourself hardly seem to feel."   Again an irrepressible bitterness crept into the speaker's tone. "You go, and come, and meet with people——"

"Aye, to be sure, I meet with people." Mr. Lambert smiled complacently. "That reminds me, I met that nice fellow, Wycliffe, again to-day, and he was so friendly and pleasant I asked him to call. I told him he must come to dinner."

"Papa! To dinner?"

"He accepted at once. Said he didn't know many people in Town at this time of year; only chanced to be up on business."

"And you asked him to dinner? And you *know* we can't have dinner-parties——"

"Pho! pho! Who talked of dinner-parties?"

Then the torrent burst forth.

"You tell me to keep the house-keeping down, and every week it is all I can *do* to pay the books. I never have *a farthing* over; and here is a man to whom we owe nothing, whom I have never even seen——''

"You will see him; he is to call first."

"Why should he call? Why should he come near us?" cried she, excitedly. "We are not the sort of people he imagines. He hears of a good house, and you invite him in an offhand manner, and he expects a gay family, a smart household, and a fine, well-set-out dinner; and—and —when he comes, there—there—is only *me!*" Her shrill young voice quavered and broke at the word. Ere he could reply she had pushed past, and vanished through the open door.

"This housekeeping mania really gets upon her nerves," said Mr. Lambert, raising his eyebrows, and shaking his head sagaciously. Nothing ever got upon his nerves.

When we are at a low ebb it is seldom that anything happens to cheer us; oftener far, some small worry takes the opportunity for making its presence known, or some blow from an unexpected quarter, falls. Caroline's "worry" had its innings first, starting with the break of day. A servant was ill, and the others considerately waited to inform their young mistress of the fact till their master had left the house, by which means the burden, with all its concomitants, was (as burdens usually were in that house) thrown on her shoulders. It had to be carried— she carried it. By afternoon the doctor had pronounced the case one for a hospital; and in place of the respectable cook, hitherto one of her young mistress' few comforts, their reigned below stairs a charwoman, upon whom, but for the pressure of necessity, she would have looked askance.

She was just considering what

was to be done next, when, with
a loud peal of the front-door
bell, the "blow" took possession of
the field. This consisted of a letter
from her godmother, and a parcel;
the former explaining that the latter
—Lina's Christmas present — had
been sent thus early, owing to the
donor's departure for wintering in a
warmer clime.

Now on this very impending
departure my hapless heroine had
been innocently building. Once
before it had happened that when
starting betimes for the Riviera, her
relation had found no opportunity
for selecting her annual gift, and
had substituted a cheque; and "If
only she would do so again," had been
the subject of many anxious musings.

But alas! here was a handsome,
useless, expensive toy, which Lady
Beaumont thought "so clever," and
would help "to amuse the children
on winter evenings."

Poor, poor Lina! She almost dashed the fiddling Neapolitan with his basket of mock fruits to the floor. She spurned him with her foot as he lay grinning there. Five pounds!— five precious golden sovereigns, that would have been—what would they not have been to her?—to be thus cruelly, wantonly, mercilessly flung away!

And presently, in the dusk—for the light was waning and the lamps were lit outside—hot, blinding tears welled unheeded from her eyes, and streamed over the hand on which her burning cheek was pressed. She must be miserable; who could say she ought not to be miserable? Who could rebuke her for giving way at last beneath such an accumulation of calamities shared by none?

And anon arose from out the last bitter reflection a still more bitter resolution. Why should her griefs be shared by none? Why should not her father for once be forced into sympathy, and have his eyes opened to the hardships of his lot and hers? He ought to feel, as she never could make him feel, that it was one deserving of resentment and rebellion. She would tell him so now; tell him the truth in plainest terms before he could stop her; before any qualms of filial duty could bind her tongue.

Hark! there was the door-bell! To her excited imagination its harsh, discordant clang sounded like a war-note to battle! It was the time of Mr. Lambert's usual return, and the next thing would be his brisk, alert entrance and cheerful greeting.

Cheerfulness at the moment was an actual crime to one whose heart was as heavy as Lina Lambert's; and scarce had the door opened and the expected step sounded on the floor, than, without raising her head or changing the crouching attitude

into which she had sunk, the piteous
outcry made itself heard, which was
to arouse at least some spark of
fellow-feeling, if it could do nothing
else, within her parent's breast.

"Papa, you wonder to find me
crying? I dare say you think I have
nothing to cry for? You often tell
me how well I am off compared with
others, and you never will see that
there are things besides food, and
clothes, and a roof over one's head;
and that it is hard, it *is* hard, to see
so much that is just beyond one's
reach at every turn. You say we are
not so very poor, but I say we *are*
poor, and it seems as if ours were almost the worst kind of poverty—oh,
don't speak!" catching an indistinct
sound which she took to be a protest.
"Don't speak; for I can't bear it. I
know what you would say perfectly
well. You would tell me it is very
wrong to be so 'ungrateful to Provi-
dence,' and so 'discontented with my

home.' You think it is all for myself that I care. But it is not. I
know it is not. It is for dear little
Florrie and Gladdie, too, whom I
have to refuse continually when
they ask for things I know they
ought to have. And they are such
dear children, and I do love them
so; I can't bear it."

Again an interruption was attempted, but again Caroline held
up a passionate, imperative hand.

"Oh, do be quiet, and don't say I
am 'undutiful' and 'disrespectful.'
I don't mean to be; but to-day I feel
as if I must speak out. Everything
has gone wrong to-day. I thought
we were at our lowest pass before,
but now here is the cook ill and gone
off to a hospital. And that," suddenly swerving round towards the
toy, with its box and wrappings,
which lay by her side, "*that* is Lady
Beaumont's Christmas present! Yes,
indeed it is! And you know what I

had thought, what I hoped it might
be.   Papa, I feel that if you have
asked that man—that Mr. Wycliffe
—to dinner, it would be the last drop
in the cup!   Papa, I cannot have
him; I *will* not!—"

"Ahem."

This time it is a protest too resolute and significant to be borne
down.   Furthermore, it was uttered,
as she for the first time perceived,
in an unknown voice.

"Papa!"

Papa?   It was—it must be her
father who was standing there in the
flickering firelight; who had entered
unannounced through the folding
doors, and made his way in silence
till he reached the point at which
she had lifted up her voice to arrest
further progress and command
attention.

It could not, dared not, be any
one else, before whom had been
poured forth the pent-up flood—the

outpourings of a sore and angry heart.

It could not be a stranger—and, oh, worst of all! most frightful, most incredible of all! *the* stranger. The very man whose name had been— horror of horrors! the head and front, the centre, the apex of her denunciation.

"Papa?" She trembled from head to foot. Involuntarily she clung to the illusion, but the hoarse, faltering accents betrayed their own uncertainty.

Slowly she left her seat, and staggered upright; and then it seemed as though some one else, not herself, had risen, and was holding by the back of the low chair, confronting with a stupefied gaze a tall figure which should have been different, absolutely, unmistakably different from what it was.

Foolishly she wondered why it should still wear an overcoat, and hold its hat in its hands. The figure that should have been, was wont to disencumber itself of both in the hall below. Besides it, the other, would have greeted her, chidingly, it might be, but yet in proper paternal fashion. It would not have stood mute, stock-still, with a sealed face and rigid outline.

It was she herself who made the first motion in the stony silence and frozen immobility of the scene. She attempted something; she knew not what.

Probably it was to escape the hideous instant of re-animation by one swift rush; to be gone ere she could be overtaken by it?

But treacherous Nature refused her aid. Her knees shook, the floor seemed to sink from beneath her feet. Like a vengeful giant the apparition of the stranger loomed between her and safety, seemed to tower overhead, to approach nearer, to bend closer—and then—one last conscious sensation, she was being caught in arms that she was power-less to shake off.

·   ·   ·   ·   ·   ·   ·

"Ha, Wycliffe? Glad to see you here." Mr. Lambert, genial and cordial, greeted his guest an hour later. "Lina, you should have had up some tea, Or, better still, stay to dinner, now you are here?" turning again to the visitor. "We dine at seven; keep early hours, you see, and are quite by ourselves to-night. If you will stay and take pot-luck——"

"Thank you. I shall be very glad to stay."

But he would not stay as he was; he would go home and change, and re-appear in correct dress, with a flower in his button-hole, and a smile in his heart.

A strange experience. Wycliffe had never known its equal. Never felt anything like the thrill of pity, tenderness, and anxiety with which he had watched the first dawnings of re-awakened life in the fair young form of which he had involuntarily taken possession, as it swayed and slipped from its foothold, and, but for him, would have fallen on the floor.

After the first pang of natural alarm and consternation, he had not pined for interference in the part allotted to him. He had gently borne his fair burden to a neighbouring sofa; laid her thereon; and then, in default of other restoratives, placed upon her brow her own handkerchief wet with her own tears.

Poor little weeper! He had sat down and scanned the pale face upon the pillow; and almost smiled, recalling the moment which had at first, it must be owned, sent an electric shock through his own veins, but which now, within the last sixty seconds, had by some magical meta-

morphosis, been transformed into a
pathetic memory.

Almost ere her eyelids had un-
closed he had felt the language of
imploring penitence in the gaze
turned upon him. He had returned
it with a look of encouragement.
Then the penitent had struggled to
draw herself upright. This he had
forbidden sternly. Then she had
striven to speak. This also had been
forbidden. Finally, he had laid his
hand on hers, and in slow, soothing
accents, as one who would compose
and comfort a bewildered child, had
spoken. Gracious powers! how he
had spoken! Looking back upon
the scene it seemed to him as though
he had been inspired. Where was
diffidence? Where embarrassment?
Surely his position ought to have
been awkward enough in having to
confess that he had not only hearkened, however involuntarily, to confidences meant for another, but had

actually heard himself alluded to as a principal ingredient in a cup whose bitterness had caused floods of tears.

And yet he was sure, positive, that he had experienced no sense of vexation, no confusion of spirit, whilst engaged in the absorbing task.

He had been bent upon reassuring and consoling. As soon as she was able, he had allowed his patient (using the term with an air of medical authority) to tell her own tale, and listened to her broken explanations and stammering apologies with perfect patience, nay, with scarcely an interruption. He saw that it relieved her to make a full confession.

And by-and-by a compact had been entered into between the two. No one was to be told what had happened; not another human being was to be cognisant of Lina Lambert's awful misdemeanour, and its still more appalling sequel. It must remain forever a secret between them; never to be alluded to, and if possible to be obliterated from the very memory of each.

Lina had been the speaker, the arranger, the dictator; all he had had to do was to promise implicit obedience.

With a seriousness equal to her own he had taken the vows. She had then proceeded: would Mr. Wycliffe give his solemn word that he would not presume. upon his knowledge of the secret? Would he, for her sake, (she had been near crying again as she spoke), for her sake, would he not now refuse the hospitality he had openly heard himself begrudged? She could never do away with the shocking fact that he *had* heard it; never cease to feel the shame of that terrible moment; but he could at least assure her of his forgiveness by affording her an opportunity of — of —. He had

gravely protested he would grant
the opportunity.

At last Lina had looked at him.
For the first time since the beginning of the interview, she had let slip
a shy glance of curiosity, and he had
fancied, though it might have been
only fancy, that speech came more
readily thereafter. But there was
not much time to improve the advance, if advance there were; for
the next ten minutes, and just as a
quiet conversation had been entered
into, designed to show that the inti-
macy begun under such unfortunate
auspices might now be proceeded
with more happily, the interruption
occurred whose anticipation had
given rise to the whole. The master
of the house, who had been detained
later than usual at his office, made
his appearance, and greeted his
daughter's visitor in the manner we
have already heard. Without hesitation, and without so much as a

side glance, Wycliffe had met the test, and responded to it as we also know.

With an inward sense of deep-breathed exultation he now made ready for the evening in store. He was conscious of standing on the brink of his fate. Perhaps for the first time in his life he had now a chance of making his way on his own merits with a pretty, charming, natural, and lovable girl. Hitherto he had been too heavily weighted.

But from his first haphazard encounter with Mr. Lambert, it had been obvious that he was being taken merely as a pleasant fellow, of whose position and fortune his new acquaintance was entirely ignorant. The ignorance amused Wycliffe; once or twice he had chuckled inwardly on finding it taken for granted that he was some insignificant unit in the great working hive,

and at its being hinted, kindly and
artlessly, that he was, perchance, an
unsuccessful one.

Upon this he had ventured further,
and cultivated Mr. Lambert's inti-
macy, always carefully keeping his
own secret. He liked the little,
cheery, volatile man who so unsus-
piciously bade him to his dreary
house. That it must be a dreary
house he knew; a dull, dingy residence in a vile situation. But somehow his feet had carried him thither
unaccountably, in spite of himself,
as it were; and he now looked back
upon the impulse with an almost
superstitious reverence.

It was no longer to him as if he
were about to revisit an ordinary
house in a common street, for the
sake of passing an uneventful evening with two every-day acquaint-
ances. No, he was going to see
her, and what that meant to Barring-
ton Wycliffe he alone knew. A

glamour was cast over the present; the future shone beneath a halo.

But to all outward seeming the next few hours passed as unremarkably as hours could do. The fair young hostess was shy, serious, and restrained, yet gentle, and responsive withal. The host was animated and easy; the guest, perhaps a shade more earnest in his endeavours to please than so simple an occasion might have seemed to warrant.

But then, "Poor fellow, I dare say he doesn't often dine out," nodded Mr. Lambert to himself; "and though it's not much of a dinner, still it is nicely set out, and Lina has been a good girl, and done her best. Anyhow, it must be better to put your feet under a gentleman's mahogany than to grub in lodgings, or snatch your food in the clatter of a restaurant."

He rejoiced to perceive no sign of sullenness in his daughter's face.

On the contrary, although she often
sat with downcast eyes, and her
speech was lower and more hesitating than its wont, he could not but
fancy that Wycliffe had no fault to
find.   He felt proud of his girl; she
had never shown to greater advantage.   It ended in his pluming himself upon his own cleverness; he
would know how to manage in
future; the way with Lina was to
whack out an invitation before her
face when she was powerless to
gainsay it.   That done, she was all
the better afterwards for a cheerful
evening.

Then his self-congratulation proceeded.   Poor little Florrie and
Gladdie had been allowed to come
down, dressed in their best, and
frolic about the drawing-room before dinner; and it was a nice
change for them.   Wycliffe must
have seen what a pretty picture it
made, the two fair-haired little

things clinging about their elder
sister, and their evident devotion to
her.   They had exhibited their little
painted men and carts, and Wycliffe
had gone down on the floor to assist
at the performance.

He had told them he had no little
sisters, and they had commiserated
his hard case.   They had demanded
to know if he had no sisters at all.

No, he had none at all.

"Not even a Lina?" said little
Gladys, twining her fingers fondly
round her sister's, and looking first
with adoring gaze upwards, and then
dolefully at the sisterless, destitute
new friend.   "Well, we wouldn't
like to give you our Lina, you
know," and she shook her head with
significant emphasis; "we couldn't
possibly spare you our Lina."
The little speaker had turned very
red, because every one laughed, and
Lina said quickly that it was the
children's bed-time.

Lina had blushed, as was natural, and the blush had not been lost upon her father, nor, he opined, upon another pair of eyes either. He fancied that Wycliffe's gaze rested a full minute on his daughter's abashed and half-averted countenance.

The awkwardness passed, however, by the latter's putting in his word for the revocation of the nursery edict, and in the end the little pair had trotted joyously off, consoled by promises of chocolate-boxes, and divers other whispered visions of delight.

It was not until just before the close of the evening—and it did not close early, we may be sure—that the guest found himself to all intents and purposes once more alone with his young entertainer. In a party of three it is not easy to let fall asides, more especially when these resolve themselves into a question to which an answer is imperatively demanded. But at length Opportunity, ever kind to the youngest of her devotees, beckoned Wycliffe, and he made haste to embrace her.

Lina was standing by the distant piano, putting up her music, her eyes large and soft, a bright tint upon either cheek.

"I am going to encroach," murmured a voice in her ear. She started; then listened with beating heart, and poor attempt at unconcern. "You made me promise to forget what I heard and saw today," said Wycliffe, slowly. He had turned his back upon the room, and was leaning over the piano towards her. "May I dare now to ask—to be allowed—to remember it?"

"Remember it?"

"All unwittingly, I unlocked a treasure," continued he, gazing at her with steadfast, longing eyes. "I had but one peep, and now I crave for more. We might have known each other, as other people do, superficially, artificially, on the surface, for months and years without having learned as much"—he corrected himself—"without *my* having learned as much of you yourself, of your real, true self, as was revealed to me in one flash this afternoon. That terrible moment! It is no longer terrible to me. Is it to you? And I can't forget it. And I know I never shall. Is it too presumptuous to hope that it may be the beginning——?" He paused for a response.

None came.

"At any rate, absolve me from my promise," he whispered; and caught the shadow of a monosyllable, and took it for an absolution.

. . . .

"Well, now, you see what I did for you!" cried Lina's · father, radiant, a month later. "There

were you moaning and groaning,
and declaring we were too poor
even to have a friend come and dine
with us! Quite annoyed because I
had asked this very Wycliffe, who
I thought would be glad of a meal,
and who now turns out to be as rich
as Crœsus! Quite in a state because
I had asked him to a family dinner!
I must say you did the civil to him
when he came; but he little knew
what I had had to go through before-
hand on his account. Phew! There
was a regular hail-storm! And if I
had known who and what Wycliffe
really was, I confess I should never
have dared to risk an invitation—
that is the joke of it! I thought he
was a mere waif and stray; cast
ashore and stranded in this great,
cold-blooded London; whom it
would be charity to——"

"Dear papa, you were always so
kind-hearted."

"Aye, aye! It is 'dear papa' now,

is it? And I am 'kind-hearted' now,
am I? But I rather think it was
only a week or two ago that I was all
that was reckless and extravagant."

"Papa, I am sorry I ever said or
thought so. I was unhappy and
over-anxious."

"So you were, my girl; so you
were. But now it is all right, and
your poor little harassed mind may
be easy at last. You have a glorious
future before you—the best fellow
in the world for your husband, and
his fine country-seat for your home.
A lucky girl you are, to be sure!
But now, my dear," added the little man, with a soberer look on his
kindly face, "just one word, Lina,
and don't take it amiss. You have
got rid of the *house-books*—at least
of any worry connected with them;
it will be all smooth sailing in that
quarter now, I fancy;—but remember, dear girl, that by-and-by there
will be other cares and crosses—no

life is without them—and when these come, try not to fret and pine; resolve not to brood over trials and vexations; set yourself *with your face to the sun*, Lina, my darling; think of the blessings, not of the shortcomings of your lot; and see that you honour your God and do credit to His service by rendering it with a cheerful heart."

His daughter kissed him silently. She had never understood her father before.

"As for me, I must do the best I can without you," proceeded he, in a lighter tone; "but I can always get along, you know. And Wycliffe has a post in his eye for me; but it is not to be talked about at present. Anyhow, the tide has turned for both of us—I said it would. As for the poor little lassies, I expect they feel as if heaven had opened, such wonderful things happen to them every day, and they are already talking of high times at 'Lina's home.' So, my dear, I give you joy, and I think you have the fairest prospect of the wish being fulfilled that ever woman had."

But he never knew, for no one ever told him—it remained, and continued to remain, a secret between the lovers, too sacred to be divulged to any one—that the whole structure of their love and happiness had been built upon the grim foundation-stone of "a terrible moment."

JEMIMA: A METAMORPHOSIS

Jemima:
A Metamorphosis

❧ ❧ ❧

Miss Jemima Sillacombe frankly owned that she did not like to be "put out of her way." Very few people who have "ways" do.

And as there are still fewer individuals of either sex who, having entered upon their fourth decade of existence, are not possessed of these early harbingers of maturity—especially when the soil has been favourable for their development — it follows that there is a vast crop of small idiosyncrasies, fancies, and foibles flourishing in the world, which are harmless enough in themselves, but which often exert an extraordinary influence on human life.

In the case of Jemima Sillacombe,
no one ever thought of denying that
Jemima had her share—and a little
more—of this unknown quantity.
As a matter of fact, she was to the
manner born.   Method, punctuality,
order, routine—these were the very
breath of her nostrils.

But then, if a lady who has lived
in the same house, in the same
style, with the same surroundings
and general environment for thirty
summers, may not be allowed to
cherish her own little "ways," and
map out her own little days, and rise
and dress, and drive and dine, and
potter about among her birds and
flowers, exactly how and when she
pleases, who may?

Jemima hurt nobody.   Defrauded
nobody.   Nay, she was an excellent,
pious creature, whose ear was ever
open to the cry of the needy, whose
heart was true, and whose life was
pure,—and no one who knew Miss

Sillacombe had ever a hard word for her.

As we have said, she still lived on in the home of her childhood, the only unwedded member of a large family, and also the youngest. From the age of twenty she had been practically in possession of both house and mother, and the pleasant, easy existence then inaugurated, had flowed on ever since.

There was really nothing to ruffle it.

Mrs. Sillacombe, an ample dowager, whose husband had been dead so long that she had almost forgotten what it was not to be a widow, was just the person for whose comfort a daughter could be properly solicitous without any very severe strain on her own. When Jemima had written dear mamma's notes, reminded her of her medicine, and read aloud to her the chief items of the Court Circular column of the

morning paper, she had performed
the principal daughterly functions of
the day.   It only remained to hold
an occasional consultation as to calls
and shopping, and to inquire what
books should be exchanged at the
circulating library.

Mrs. Sillacombe saw everything
through Jemima's eyes,—or, to be
more correct, saw all she cared to
see.   Nothing beyond the range of
her house, her servants, her meals,
her daily drive, and her occasional
doctor's visit, had any real hold on
her attention.   Even the affairs of
her married daughters—she had no
sons—elicited but a flickering and
uncertain interest; and if a more
than ordinarily startling piece of gossip were brought to her ken, and she
were sufficiently roused to put a
question or two, and pass a comment
on the replies received, Jemima
would delightedly exclaim that "dear
mamma was quite excited."

To be plain, the old lady led a stupid, animal existence; and only the genuine sweetness of her daughter's nature could have cast over it any sort of halo.

Jemima was, however, perfectly content. She had never known her mother different; she had never known much of her sisters at all; she felt no lack, had no unsatisfied yearnings.

On the contrary, it seemed to her that she was one of the luckiest persons imaginable, in that she was still an inmate of the beautiful, old, well-appointed domain; still supported in her authority by the grey-headed butler and house-keeper, who had come in her infancy; could still step into the high-swung barouche as regularly as three o'clock came round every afternoon, and, with parcels, books, and letters piled upon the front seat, roll off in state to call at one familiar door after another,—and still, on her return at the accustomed hour, note no other change than what the seasons brought in the scene which met her eyes, as the drawing-room door opened on the cheerful tea-table and kindly urn ready waiting.

But extend her drive, or take tea elsewhere? Not she! Not Jemima Sillacombe!

She put it upon her mother; but dear mamma would have eaten her muffin peacefully enough half an hour later, if it had been suggested to make a détour on the homeward path. No; it was Jemima herself whose watch came out by instinct as the light began to wane on an autumn afternoon, and who would out with the order "Home" before Mrs. Sillacombe could be heard on behalf of a neglected parcel still on the seat opposite.

The parcel could be left another day, Jemima would affirm, wrapping

herself briskly in her driving-cloak.
It was too late to do more that
day.

Jemima had an hour for everything, and a season for everything.
Five minutes with her was a very
much longer period than five minutes with most people.

Then she always knew exactly
where she ought to be upon the
staircase when Thomas issued forth
from the back regions to roll the
gong for dinner, and what she
should be doing when he was heard
placing the bedroom candles in the
anteroom, preparatory to the night's
rest. She remembered on what
days the housemaids reigned su-
preme in their several rooms,—she
never invited people to dine on
Thursdays, devoted to special plate-
cleaning in the pantry,—and she
would not have kept coachman and
footman out beyond their own tea
hour for the world.

"The kindest, consideratist young lady as ever was," Hubbard, the butler, would declare—in proof of which he would loftily abstract the newspaper from under Jemima's very nose. But a young and pert housemaid was heard to cry shrilly back on one occasion, "Lor', she ain't nothen but an old maid born," which made Hubbard very angry indeed.

"I declare, Jemima, I think you are the most enviable person in the world." The speaker was Jemima's eldest sister, a matron of forty-five, who had early left the nest, and was now every inch the mother of a family and mistress of a household. "You are always so cool and comfortable," proceeded Lady Franklin, fanning herself, for she was stout, and the warm weather tried her severely, "and you seem to have time for everything, while I am in a 'drive' from morning till midnight.

And there is Lenny's tea-party this afternoon," she subjoined in an aggrieved tone, which might have been interpreted, "That is the last straw."

"To be sure. His birthday party." Jemima nodded cheerful comprehension. "I am coming, Caroline."

"*Are* you? So good of you." Lady Franklin paused and hesitated. "I don't know how I am ever to get it in, I am sure. I did promise the child, but I did not take in that it meant. my flying home after the lecture, and we are dining out, and—"

"You gay person!"

"Indeed, I am not gay, but I am so hurried and worried. Jemima, if I *should* be late—you know what lectures are—they *will* go on and on, and the Dewhursts are particularly anxious to introduce Professor Grimsel afterwards—that is the real reason of my going—could you,

would you mind, if I were not
there, sitting down with the children and pouring out tea? I *mean*
to be back, of course; only, if I am
not——"

"You can depend on me. Don't
trouble about it, Caroline. I have
arranged to be at your house by
four o'clock, and——"

"And that means you will be
there." The elder lady's brow
cleared, and she gave a sigh of
relief. "Lucky you! You have no
one to throw all your plans into confusion at the last moment, as mine
are a dozen times in a week. *You*
can go and come as you choose.
Well, it is something off my mind, at
any rate, to know that if I *am* late—
you are such a favourite that Lenny
will be quite satisfied if I say Aunt
Jemima is .due at four o'clock for
certain—and—and it doesn't put you
out of your way?" having now a
moment for the afterthought.

"Not at all out of my way. I have kept it in my mind ever since you told me you were giving the party; and the carriage is to be round half an hour earlier than usual, and dear mamma is quite pleased to lunch a little tiny bit sooner in order to be ready. Then I am to be dropped at the Grange as we drive home, and Thomas will bring the pony-cart for me at six, so that I shall just get home in time to dress for dinner."

A twinkle in the other's eye was lost upon the speaker. ("Goodness gracious! To hear her!" Lady Franklin was saying to herself, betwixt contempt and a species of envy, "she might have been going to Court and a State ball afterwards, for all the forethought bestowed!") "You have certainly a genius for organisation, Jemima," observed she, drily.

"I do like to have things fit in,"

Jemima bridled, with modest elation, "and it is quite easy by just giving one's mind to it."

"Humph!"

"I don't speak for you, Caroline. In a household like yours there must be many interruptions and hindrances. But with me," the spinster proceeded, complacently, "it is quite different. I have only dear mamma to consider; and really our servants are so good, and understand our ways so thoroughly——"

"I know—I know. Everything goes on oiled wheels. You roll through life on easy cushions." Lady Franklin evinced a momentary impatience. "And you always look so trim and smart," glancing down at herself, and again back at the fresh, flowering muslin which made her own far handsomer dress look dusty and shabby. "I really have had no time to think about summer clothes,—but you are always in the van. I said yesterday, when I saw the first light bonnet in the street— I was inside Atkinson's and I just saw the bonnet, not the carriage, through the fallals in the window—I said to Wynnie, 'That must be Aunt Jemima.' "

"Too bad of you. I am sure I am not a great dresser."

"It isn't that. No; I don't think you dress more than other people. We all get the things in the long-run—only, you are the first. You have the time to attend to it, and to notice that the season is here. There you are now, in that pretty muslin—and it is very becoming, Jemima—you can wear a muslin still—I wish *I* could. A great hot silk—I wonder if I could not have a muslin made a little elaborately, just for the very warm days? I shall ask Miss Johnston; she is such a good dressmaker, she could—But I must not run on, I have a thousand things

to do. You are not going out this
morning?''

"Only to the garden. The roses
are ready for cutting——''

"Cutting roses? How old fash-
ioned and leisurely it sounds! Dear
me, if *my* roses were to wait till I
had time to cut them——''

"Yours are wasted, Caroline. I
always lament when I go to your
rose garden that no one thinks of
drying them for the rooms——''

"My dear, who should think?''
Again the elder sister manifested a
certain pettishness. "Who in our
house has time for those fiddy-faddy
businesses? *I* haven't. The girls
are at their lessons, the servants at
their work. If we have visitors,
they want to be taken here, there,
and everywhere. It is only you, you
fortunate mortal, you petted-by-the-
gods Jemima Sillacombe, who can
take into your scheme of life even
the preservation of the crumpled

rose-leaf, which is not allowed to disturb the surface of your bed of down."

Laughing, and kissing her sister affectionately, Lady Franklin, with recovered good-humour, rustled away; and Jemima, having first restored to its place an antimacassar which had been caught on the point of the departing parasol, and otherwise smoothed down disarrangements—for Caroline never failed to leave disarrangements, to the orderly eye—picked up her basket and scissors, and tripped off to her congenial occupation among the flower borders.

She had been detained for half an hour; but then, she always reckoned on such a chance detention; so told herself, with a sense of being sisterly and indulgent, that it did not put her out of her way, for one must always take into account a married sister living within a few miles in a country neighbourhood.

"I don't suppose Jemima will ever marry," cogitated the latter, as she consulted her watch at the same moment as Jemima smoothed out the antimacassar; "she is far too well off as she is. Nothing to worry her, no one to interfere with her; no cares, no troubles, no anxieties. Even when our mother is taken from us—and that we need not anticipate for long enough, with her good health, and easy, regular life; still, she must go some day—but even then Jemima will reign on here happily enough. She will be quite able to afford it; and with the old servants about her, and us so near, and so many neighbours besides, she need never feel lonely. One of us sisters could always spare her a girl to stop with her, if it came to that; or Matilda would come for good, if wanted. She has her poor people, too, and her parish interests; and is on such good terms with everybody

round that, upon my word, most
people would consider her the
luckiest creature alive. And I fancy
she would call herself so." A
pause. Then, "I wonder, now—I
wonder if a single woman like
Jemima really *is* lucky?" cogitated
the matron, as a softer expression
stole across her brow. "She always
appears to be absolutely content
and serene. Yet, looking at the
case dispassionately, it seems, if one
were to speak plainly, rather a
selfish sort of happiness. Not that
poor, dear Jemima *is* selfish, only
she knows no better, and is so
entrenched in her own funny little
state, that—well, well, it can't be
helped. And I don't know what
possesses me to think there is anything that needs help, when I am
always pretending to envy my sister's easy lot, and sometimes do
actually, at the moment, believe my
own words! I wonder, now——?"

But she soon forgot to wonder.   Her own multifarious concerns, which for the moment had been in abeyance, were again buzzing about her like so many flies, and shut out every other point of the landscape. As usual, she was late in arriving at her little son's birthday party.

The party was in full swing, and a tremendous chattering and laughing sounded through the open door of the room in which it was assembled.

"That cannot be only Jemima," swiftly concluded Jemima's sister. The next minute—"Oh, Bobby!" she exclaimed, in surprise, recognising in Sir William's youngest brother the author of the merriment. "When did you arrive? We had no idea you were in England."

Captain Franklin chuckled like a boy. "No more has any one else, my dear. Hold hard. Give us a fraternal salute," kissing the matronly cheek, which blushed

beneath the unaccustomed tribute.
"I have been kissing 'em all round,"
proceeded the sailor, triumphantly.
"Had to, to find out which were my
nieces and which weren't.   Crime
first—punishment afterwards."

"But he didn't kiss Auntie Jem,
and she was the only one he missed
out," the hero of the day shouted
from his birthday seat of honour
with the full force of his seven-year-
old lungs, an announcement which
really seemed in a measure necessary. "And he's brought me a par-
rot and a tortoise, and he says——"

"He's going to dance a hornpipe," broke in a still shriller
treble, "and he says——"

"He's going to take us all to the
Circus," a third took up the cry,
"and he says——"

"And he says," appeared to be the
catch-word.

Lady Franklin strove in vain to
be heard above the tumult; she

wanted to be hospitable, genial, welcoming, but she had no chance of being anything. And there was Jemima, too—the din must be absolutely deafening to poor Jemima!

A vision of the dainty figure in its crisp flounces and frills, framed by the large, solemn, massively-furnished drawing-room, which had been present to her mind's eye by fits and starts all through the intervening hours, stood out clearly at the moment. She felt as if she must rescue her gentle, bewildered, little old maid of a sister from this pandemonium.

Tea was over, and she could at least suggest an adjournment. "You are terribly hot in here, and I see you have finished; will not some of you like to come to another room, or——"

"Uncle Bobby is going to dance a hornpipe." A dozen small voices rang forth together like a peal of bells; while Uncle Bobby himself, big, brown-bearded, jolly, and sunburnt, beamed acquiescence.

"How   kind!   But   perhaps Jemima——"

"Aunt Jem wants to see the hornpipe as much as any of us." And Aunt Jem smiled assent.

"You poor dear!" murmured Lady Franklin, aside. "Sailors have such overpowering spirits," she added later, putting her hand to her forehead.

"Quite delightful," responded Jemima, as though she had been called upon to acclaim.

Lady Franklin looked at her. "Oh, I did not mean *that*. Yes, of course. Sir William always says Bobby makes him laugh more than any one. But I do wish—Bobby's voice is so *very* loud, and his laugh is perfectly *stentorian*, and he never minds *who* is here, or *what* he does, —but of course I know he is a dear

fellow, and as good as gold, and has
the kindest heart in the world. But,
my dear Jemima, I did feel for you.
I am sure if my head aches, yours
must be ten times as bad. And
after your putting yourself out to
come, and we all know you don't like
to be put out of your way——"

"No, no; I am going to convoy
Miss Jemima home." A voice in
the rear—a frank, bold, confident
voice—made both ladies start as if it
had been a pistol-shot.

"I'm coming back, you ruffians,"
continued the same speaker, as the
swarming crew were shaken off a big
central figure, and Captain Franklin
emerged to view. "You'll have
enough of me, never fear. I'll give
you some fun before I'm done with
you; but sheer off now. Miss
Jemima, it is long since we've met,
but we are relations all the same, or
what amounts to the same thing—
you must let me see you across the

fields; it is such a jolly evening for a walk, and that fellow"—lowering his tone, and eyeing a young and callow footman who had been sent to escort his mistress home, and who was now endeavouring to assume the correct statuesque attitude with only indifferent success—"he can be dispensed with, can't he? We don't want him, do we? 'Tis ever so much pleasanter walking than driving; may I tell him to trot off again?"

"Good heavens! What an odd couple!" cried Lady Franklin, to the group who stood looking after the pair that started presently. "Poor Jemima! There was no way out of it. I could hardly help laughing at her look of utter confusion. She who never sees a man—far less talks to one—what must she feel to find herself let in for a two-mile walk all alone with such an extraordinary specimen of the genus sailor as Bob?"

"Now, do tell me, Jemima, what

you found to talk about, and how you got on," demanded she the next day, having driven over on purpose. "Bobby declared you got on 'like a house on fire.' But then, he always 'gets on like a house on fire' with everybody, and imagines every one else does the same. He is such a rattle——"

"I don't think you should call him a rattle, Caroline."

"*Not?* Not a boisterous, blustering——"

"He can talk most sensibly and agreeably. As soon as we were alone," proceeded Jemima, with animation, "he quite dropped his jokes and—and chaff; and I assure you I never met with any one who—that is to say, we found plenty of subjects in common, and we agreed upon some of them, and, when we did not, I was quite willing to be corrected, for he has seen more of life than I——"

"That is not saying *very* much, is it?   However, I am glad if your ignorance came in handy on the occasion.   I have always heard that any and every kind of knowledge is sure to come in useful at some time or other, but I never knew before that *want* of it would.   So Bobby instructed you?   On what points?"

"Ever so many.   What a wonderful career he has had!   And how much he has seen and done!   I do think a sailor's must be a most interesting life.   We were looking at the Cathedral tower——"

"The Cathedral tower?   From where did you see the Cathedral tower?"

"From—from the Beacon Hill," faltered Jemima; then gathered courage and proceeded: "I hope, Caroline, that I did not do anything impru — unconventional — I   mean anything I ought not, in walking round the Beacon with your brother-in-law. Of course, if I had been a girl—but at my age, and he is over forty—and Sir William's brother—it seemed to me it would have been ridiculous if I had made an objection when Captain Franklin proposed it. I did hesitate, and then his evident wonder and absolute unconsciousness of having suggested anything unusual showed me at once that it would be quite silly to make a fuss.''

"Of course." Lady Franklin smiled a little to herself. ("Make a fuss, indeed! Poor dear thing! She is actually blushing! What a perfect innocent she is!") "Now, Jemima, there is something I want to ask you to do for me. I drove over at this unearthly hour on purpose; I knew you would not have stirred out of doors yet. Well, now, listen to me, there's a dear. I am taking Bob to the lawn-tennis party at the Worthingtons this afternoon

—I had not meant to go, but his turning up so unexpectedly puts out all my plans, and Sir William would not like it if I were to turn him adrift. So I must sacrifice myself, as usual, and drive in exactly the opposite direction to what I had intended. But as I know you always go into Maltburgh on a Tuesday, will you call at the library and leave this list, and also this order at the butcher's, and this prescription at the chemist's? It does not matter about waiting to have it—the prescription—made up. They can send it out; only, it ought to be left early in the afternoon;" and she proceeded to enlarge.

Jemima in silence accepted the commissions. She certainly did drive into Maltburgh on Tuesdays; it was her invariable rule to do so; and any deviation from her rule would have—no, she was not prepared to deviate.

"Now, Bobby, I am going to introduce you to all the pretty girls in the neighbourhood," quoth Bobby's hostess, a few hours later, as she took her seat in an open barouche and unfurled her parasol. "Rose Hall, Thomas."

"Always ready for pretty girls," responded her companion, promptly. "And you are right to do it sharp, Caroline. A week is my limit, and then I'm off."

"Only a week?"

The sailor laughed. "A week is a week to us jack-tars. We're bound to scud through life with our topsails flying. I shall be friends with every friend of yours by the end of. my week, and—I say, I've begun already. Began yesterday · with Miss Jemima, and we're quite chummy to-day——"

"To-day? But you haven't seen her to-day?"

"Haven't I though?" Captain

Bob laughed again. "You had not quitted the field ten minutes before I was on it. We've had another walk——"

"No?"

"I strolled over to pay my respects to your mother, as I was not allowed to go in yesterday, and found your sister just starting for her round of poor people in the village. I went round with her."

"My dear Bob! With Jemima? Why, she never allows *any one* to go with her to her poor people. It must have put her dreadfully out of her way."

"I dare say it did,—but she didn't say so. I asked if she were going to this tennis party——"

"Jemima at a tennis party! I wish I had heard you. What did she say? Was she not amused?"

"Not at all. What was there to amuse? I thought everybody went to tennis parties. I thought it was the favourite, not to say the only, form of dissipation in a country place.''

''But Jemima never goes in for dissipation. I don't mean to say that she absolutely abjures tennis parties; only, if she appears at them, she stays about half an hour, keeping the carriage waiting all the time, takes a sip of tea and a stroll round the garden, and retreats before any of the real fun of the fair begins. She never goes to the Worthingtons' at all, because it is so far off. You must know that Jemima never keeps coachman and horses out beyond a certain hour; and if a house is ever so pleasant, and old Jenkyns declares—and I believe he often invents, too—that it is a mile beyond what he considers his horses can do, there is an end of the matter. Between ourselves, Jemima is the veriest old maid——''

"*Is* she?" said Bob, significantly. His eyes danced above his brown beard; he had found a stimulus hitherto wanting in his smooth career.

Five days passed, and Sunday came—a midsummer Sunday, sweet and heavy with odorous blossoms, fiercely hot in the sun, but delicious in the shade. Morning service and the early dinner which followed in Mrs. Sillacombe's well-regulated household were over, and the old lady had retired to doze in her bedroom.

Jemima had put on a cooler dress, and laid bonnet, gloves, parasol, and prayer-book on her bed, in readiness for six o'clock, at which time she would again sally forth in response to the chiming of church bells. Jemima never had her accoutrements put back in wardrobe and drawers on Sundays; her maid's services were dispensed with

till night; and she invariably laid
out the little array upon the bed in
exact parallel lines. 　　　　'

Having done so on the present
occasion, there was a slight, a very
slight, deviation from her usual
method of procedure: instead of
walking straight to the arm-chair by
the open window, as was her wont,
she made a movement, an absent-
minded movement, in the direction
of the mirror, and from her toilet-
table took up a comb. Jemima's
hair curled a little, naturally, upon
her forehead. With the tail of the
tortoise-shell comb Jemima drew
down the little curls on either side
of the parting, and poked them
about.

She then took up a hand-glass, and
deliberately examined the side view
of her head and profile.

Finally, she turned straight round
and looked at her back.

There was nothing amiss with the

back, nor yet with the ruffled frill at
the neck; while as for the hair, it
was glossy, trim, and dressed to perfection—as she esteemed perfection.
A shade too stiff it had been where
the rippling waves drew back from
the still smooth and somewhat pensive brow, but this, as we know, had
been rectified, and yet it was a full
half-hour ere the occupant of the
luxurious bedchamber quitted it,
and, gliding downstairs, passed
through a side door which opened
into the garden.

Jemima was going to read her
book out of doors. Here was inno-
vation number two within the space
of sixty minutes.

Tripping lightly through the
flower borders, scarcely distinguish-
able amidst their brilliant profusion,
Miss Sillacombe made her way to a
wooded bank which sloped towards
the west, from whence a lovely view
of the country beyond could be

obtained, including — but of that she made no account, of course — the path which any one coming from the Grange would probably traverse.

Here the little lady paused and instinctively scrutinised the rustic seat which, under the cool shade of overspreading boughs, invited a sojourn.

Jemima was not very fond of rustic benches with ragged pieces of bark protruding, to say nothing of earwigs and spiders. She would have preferred a nice clean garden chair, and could easily have carried one, or had it carried for her, from the cupboard in the hall, but she could not exactly have suggested any necessity for more than one, and such necessity might just possibly arise. She preferred to run the gauntlet of spiders and bark, and, after a moment's hesitation and a little careful arrangement of her spotless flounces, settled herself and opened her book.

A hum of insects and the tapping of a woodpecker on the dry stem of a fir tree close behind, alone fell upon her ear for some lapse of time; yet it is notable that even the snap of a dry twig or the rustle of a withered leaf caused the reader to catch her breath and bend a little lower the head, which was resolved to show it was not going to incline towards intrusive sounds. "He shall find me calmly reading," said Miss Jemima, to herself.

And at length there could be no mistake. The calmness, the decorum, the feint of entire absorption in the volume which lay upon the lady's spotless lap, were to be called into play. Steps were certainly approaching.

Pit-a-pat goes Jemima's heart. Nearer and nearer they come—so near are they now that a more wily

diplomatist would have raised a
languid eye and dreamily investi-
gated; but those of our modest
spinster were still nailed to the open
page, when, "Upon my word, my
dear sister, you are deaf as a post!"
was shouted almost into her hat
brim.

"I came through the wood," pursued Lady Franklin, dropping ex-
haustedly on the seat, which had
been brushed with a view to another
occupant. "Though it is so much
longer, it is everything to have
shade on a day like this. But if I
had known it was so hot, I should
have let Bob come instead of me, as
he offered to do. I did half let him;
only, I thought it would have put
you out of your way, as you never
do have visitors on Sundays."

She then divulged her business,
which was of the ordinary type
between sisters living in close prox-
imity, and proceeded:

"But how is it you are sitting out here? I thought you all went to sleep in your rooms on Sunday afternoons. It is not your way to——"

"My way?" For once the poor badgered Jemima turned a red cheek and a frown upon her tormentor. "To hear you talk, Caroline, one would think I was a perfect machine! Can I do nothing that is not 'my way'? I do wish"—then the speaker recollected herself. "It is not my 'way' to be cross, at any rate, is it, dear?" she smiled a little ruefully; "but, to tell the truth, you startled me just now, and you know I am not accustomed to being taken by surprise——"

"So I told Bob. I caught him sloping off in this direction, and he owned he was just going to look round here,—you know he always 'drops in' and 'looks round' on people, and never dreams of not being welcome anywhere, — and I

said, 'You will only put Jemima out
of her way,'—oh, my dear, I forgot
it vexed you to hear this,—but the
fact is, we always *do* say it.   And if
it hadn't been for me, the tiresome
fellow would have been over this
evening, just when you were starting for church!   He declared he
must say 'Good-bye,' as he is off
to-morrow,—and Goodness knows
when we shall see him again!—for
though he is leaving the Navy after
this cruise, no one has the slightest
notion where he proposes to settle
down, and it may be at the utter-
most parts of the earth,—but I said
I would carry all messages, for you
always went to church on Sunday
evenings, and would not like to be
put out of—Ha! ha! ha! I am afraid
I did say it, Jemima; and I assure
you Bob was quite as indignant as
you are.   He muttered something as
if he thought he knew better than
I about it.   Perhaps you really would

have liked him to come and say
'Good-bye'?'' she suggested, as with
a momentary afterthought.

"It—it doesn't matter, Caroline."

A low, faintly-uttered response.

"I will take any message you like,
you know."

Jemima was silent.

"Shall I wish him *Bon voyage?*"

Jemima turned away her head.

"Jemima—Jemima—shall I let
him come here to-night?"

A running tear splashed on to the
page of Jemima's book.

.   .   .   .

"Yes, go—go in, and win!" cried
Lady Franklin, waving her handkerchief in triumph to an expectant
figure, as she almost flew home,
stout and heavy as she was, ten
minutes afterwards. "Go, and God
speed you. Don't lose a minute—
not a minute. My dear Bob, I am so
glad—so happy. I can hardly speak.
What are you doing out here in the

open sun?''—for he had come half-
way to meet her in his impatience,
and was now standing open-mouthed
in the midst of a broiling, dusty
road, all unconscious of its demerits.
''Find me an ounce of shade, and I
will tell you all about it, and you
shall own I am cleverer than you
ever dreamed, and——''

''And kinder,'' cried the sailor,
seizing both her hands and wringing
them with terrific fervour. (''Oh,
my rings!'' she moaned to herself,
as they dug into her soft flesh. But
she uttered no syllable aloud.)

''But for your putting me on my
mettle,'' continued the grateful
brother, ''I don't know that the first
idea of such a thing would ever have
occurred even to my presumption.
You piqued and provoked me,
Caroline. I know now you did it on
purpose. Then, when you had prepared the ground, you let fall a
seed of hope, without which I should

never—but no matter. Out with your tale! Bless you for it! Go on with your finding your sister——"

"Sitting outside, on the edge of the wood, with a book before her *upside down!* A fact; it was. So deeply interested that she never heard me till I was looking over her shoulder! Then such a start, and such blank, instantaneous, unmistakable disappointment! It is too bad of me to reveal the secret of that dear innocent heart; and if I had not known *your* feelings——! But, my dear brother, you must never betray me. No, indeed; not through years and years to come. Jemima possesses what is a very rare treasure in these days, a real sense of delicacy; and it would be outraged —I am quite in earnest when I say this—by her knowing that I went there this afternoon for no other purpose than to spy out the land for you. We must keep our own secret

—at any rate until the wedding is over. I *thought* it was all right; but with a person like my sister I could not be sure—she was so very careful, so very anxious not to betray herself. And then, you know, I feared that from her point of view she had so much to lose."

"So she has." Captain Franklin's brow slightly clouded.

"Not a bit of it. She will gain a hundred thousand times the value of every item. Look at the two sides of the question. Would *you* put—would any true-hearted man or woman put —comfort, luxury, leisure, and an empty, barren life (for that is what it amounts to in dear Jemima's case)— against the love of a good man, the devotion of a warm, honest heart, the pleasures of companionship, the fresh sympathies and interests, the myriads of new friends, the very self-sacrifices so dear to a gentle, womanly soul?" (She had been saying this so often to herself that it now poured out as from a pent fountain - head.) "Oh, my dear Bob," cried the affectionate creature, her eye moist before the picture she had conjured up, "have no fears; there will not be a happier woman in all the countryside than your wife. You may have to live in a cottage, and jog her about in a pony-cart, and rake your own gravel, and mow your own lawn—she will find it all delightful. Her sweet nature is cramped and warped as it is; it will expand beneath your so-called privations. Jemima will grow younger every year——"

"She will—she will."

"Of course she will. Instead of rule and rhythm, starched primness and narrow-mindedness—(those are not the real fruits of Jemima's nature, only the weeds of the soil)—we shall have her joining in every freak, trotting at your heels to every

gathering, turning upside down all
her old notions,—you are the very
man for her; I long to see the day.
Away with you now; you will catch
her somewhere, somehow. I leave
it in your hands; only, if I don't see
you both come smiling in to supper
this evening——"

And in they came.

And every prediction above recorded was fulfilled to the letter.
Indeed, it was quite a joke to the
county the fashion in which Captain
and Mrs. Franklin conducted their
married life. They never did anything like other people; they never
knew where they were going or what
they were likely to be about. They
dashed hither and thither—always
together—always radiantly happy
and good-humoured—always ready
for anything and everything that
turned up. When·Jemima saw her
sister Matilda (a widow, who thank-
fully succeeded to her place as

daughter at home, only bargaining
that her children should be established there also, which Lady Franklin said was quite proper and
natural), when Jemima saw the
widow roll off in the well-known
barouche from a social gathering,
long before any one else thought of
moving, and remembered that
Matilda was now as punctilious
about servants' meals and horses'
legs as she had once been, she
chuckled to herself as she gaily
waved a parting hand; and she
smiled again broadly and contentedly
as she jogged home beneath the
moon, four or five hours later, she
and her husband having been kept
almost by force to an impromptu
supper and a merry evening. These
sort of impromptus rapidly grew to
be the most natural things in the
world, in her eyes.

When a voice would be heard peal-
ing through the small domain,

"Jemima—Jemima—get on your togs, and come for a day's outing," at the smallest possible notice, Jemima flew to obey, and flew past the clock without ever once glancing at it.

And she never troubled to inquire how or when she was to find time for this and that, which had to be done sometime. She dashed off notes instead of writing letters. She kept whole flower borders in blossom instead of snipping roses. She read newspapers and magazines, and knew what was going on in all sorts of out-of-the-way places, instead of contenting herself with the Court Circular and the leading paragraphs.

She revelled in hospitality, and Bob's friends wired they were coming down upon her to luncheon or dinner without an instant's hesitation. She walked through the mud to meet them at the station, if

Bob couldn't go and the pony was needed.

One and all agreed she was the jolliest little bride—and when the baby came——!

THE JUBILEE SEAT

The Jubilee Seat

Kent is a pleasant, sweet-smelling county to dwell in; it is also cheap and convenient for a battered old sea captain, who has done with tar and pitch and ocean waves, and has a wife and family to think of. Captain Butterworth—good old Tom, of the *Mary Jane*, who had faithfully served her owners for many a year, and was now pensioned off and rheumatic—had fancied that the ruddy woods and chalky hollows of his birthplace would suit him in more respects than one when looking about for some quiet haven in which to cast his final anchor; and he had found as snug a berth, according to himself, as ever an old decrepit salt could swing his hammock in.

In other words, he had succeeded in turning a pretty and comfortable farmhouse into as close a resemblance to a taut merchantman as masts, figureheads, and every sort of marine relic erected at intervals could. Purfoy Farm was the amusement of the neighbours, and its decoration and embellishment the very breath of old Butterworth's nostrils.

The captain himself was the only man about the place. He had a wife and several daughters, while a couple of country lasses did the rough work of the establishment; but as the worthy fellow had been shrewd enough to shut his eyes to the blandishments of agricultural agents, and positively limit his energies and his expenditure to the small garden and paddock which went with the farmhouse—permitting others to annex its hop-fields and pasture-lands—he had no need of male hands other than his own; and mowed his own grass, cut his own vegetables, and shook down the fruit from his own orchards year in and year out, with a cheery zest and independence, that it did one's heart good to see.

Inside, it is true, Mrs. Butterworth held her sway, and it was the by no means inconsiderable one of an invalid—an invalid to whom was brought every item of household intelligence, before whom every plan was laid, and without whose sanction nothing could be undertaken.

From her couch in the low parlour window, round which in summer the roses swung and clustered, the pale sweet face was ready with its smile, and the thin white hand with its wave of recognition to every passing figure, and there were two at least of the home circle who never failed to look round and shout a greeting or remark, whenever they came within range of those patient, watchful eyes.

"Ho, old girl, got you a nice bunch of turnips this morning!" The captain would pause in his trudge up the little path, put down his basket, and hold up in review its contents. ("She likes to see everything," he would say to himself.) Anon it would be, "Now, Bess, I'm off to take a turn with the mowing-machine. I sha'n't be round here for a bit yet; but you'll hear me and it going along. You'll know where we are. We start at the far end of the grass, and work this way, in and out. When you hear us stop, we shall be at the walnut tree. We turn there and go back. (She likes to hear all about it," he would nod himself off, his sunburnt face glazing gaily in the sun.)

Molly, too, remembered that her mother liked to hear about things.

Molly would bring peas and goose-
berries to shell or husk beneath the
window, and always took care to
have something on hand, which
brought her there, at what time
her father's manifold duties lay in
other directions. They arranged
this together. Ernestine, the next
daughter, was not to be depended
upon. Ernestine would promise and
forget.

Moreover, Ernestine could not see
why her mother could not sometimes
be left alone for an hour or two,
since mother herself declared she
was happy and content with her
books and work. Could she not take
a nap, if her eyes were tired?

And Ernestine did think it was
rather absurd the way in which her
father and Molly flew to the window
with every silly piece of news, however trifling; as if it could possibly
interest any one to hear that a Sunday school treat was passing along

the lane, or that the miller's cart
had broken down going over the
bridge where the two streams met!
Ernestine, or Nesta, as she was
called in the home circle, was, to tell
the truth at once, the only discordant
member of it.   The younger sisters,
the school-girls, Amy and Prilly,
were as full of spirits, as good-
humoured, amiable, and affectionate
as the jolly captain and his first-
born; but Nesta was "difficult."

"We put it down to her having
been brought up by an aunt—owing
to my being away in the West
Indies, and mother ill." This from
the worthy captain in confidence.
"We think the good lady—to be
sure, she meant well, and Nesta is
her god-daughter—but the fact remains that Mrs. Miller put ideas
into our girl's head.   Seems as if she
couldn't settle down to our small
ways and be comfortable, after the
grand house in St. George's Square.

She always harps upon London.
But Mrs. M. has girls of her own to
take about now, and Nesta don't get
asked as she used to.   Her cousins
ain't exactly handsome, d'ye see?
Well, it's not for me to say, but they
tell me—folks who ought to know
do—that Nesta is too pretty a creature to be made free of any house
full of daughters.   And she is not
just what you may call easy to get
on with.   There's Molly now—that
lassie never wants *anything* for herself.   It's always, 'Oh, that will just
do for mother,' or, 'That's the very
thing Nesta was longing for,' and
Miss Nesta takes it as if it were her
right!   Still, I am not denying she's
a pretty creature—at least, so folks
tell me"—hastily correcting himself
—"and if she had never been at
that horrid house—if Jessie Miller
had never taken her up, and put
it into her head to look down on
plain ways, and fret after finery and

tomfoolery, she would never have thought of it for herself.   But there! She's our daughter, mother's and mine, and she must have *some* stuff in her, bless her!'' the old voice would round off in a contented chirrup, and the momentary cloud which the thought of Nesta's aunt and the house in St. George's Square (to his simple mind the apex of fashion) never failed to evoke, would pass from the speaker's brow.

''It is a pity she always reads the London papers,'' said Mrs. Butterworth.

But Ernestine refused to see that any harm could come from London papers.   Her father read, and why not she?

Moreover, she took in the *Queen;* and it is safe to say that not an entertainment was given, not an engagement announced, nor a piece of society gossip chronicled that Ernestine Butterworth—albeit the

names of those concerned were to
her but names and nothing more—
did not pore over the lines, and
find in them food for envy and
desire.

And now we must proceed with
our little story.

The month was June, and the year
the recent one of glorious com-
memoration. Nothing was being
thought of or talked of but the
Diamond Jubilee, and ways and
means of viewing the Royal Progress.

"That settles it," said Captain
Butterworth, laying down paper and
spectacles at one and the same time.
"I had thought—well, I didn't see
the last Jubilee, being at sea; and
none of you girls saw it either—so I
did think that maybe if a guinea
would have done the lot——"

"A guinea!" It was Ernestine's
scornful voice which struck in. "A
guinea! Why, dear me, father, one

would suppose you never read anything, and never even heard people
talk.   The seats are to be——"

"Aye, aye, lass, hold hard; the old
man is neither so blind nor so deaf
as you think.   I know well enough—
it is plain enough here," tapping
with his glasses the outspread sheet
upon his knee, "what folks will have
to pay who want to see their Queen
on Jubilee Day, and what I say is,
that settles the question.   The sight
is not for us; not for poor people,
who haven't strength to stand in the
streets—"

"To stand in the streets!   I should
think not, indeed."

"You are as like to stand as you
are to sit, my girl," said the old captain, quietly; and took out his pipe.
An obstinate look had stolen over
his features; the lips protruded, the
shaggy eyebrows knitted themselves
together.

"It's all up now," muttered Ernes-

tine, beneath her breath.   She knew
the signs.

But although the case was desperate, she could not bring herself to
hold her tongue.

"You need not at least tantalise us
by saying what might have been,"
she cried, passionately.   "It is bad
enough, as it is.   And here is Cousin
Mat coming home from Australia—
coming, he says, on purpose to see
the Procession, and the part their
fellows take in it.   He will think it
odd that not one of us, his own relations and the only ones he has, can
even go up from here—an hour's
journey—while he crosses the ocean,
travels thousands and thousands of
miles—"

"With thousands and thousands of .
pounds to do it on.   Mat's a rich
man, I am a poor one.   He can
afford whatever he chooses; and I
think all the better of him for being
keen enough about the honour of his

colony and all that; I think he is
doing the right thing to make a dash
for the old country, and send up his
cheer for the Queen among the rest
of us."

"The rest of us?   I wish it were."

"Even though he has to start off
in a fortnight's time," pursued the
old seaman, unheeding.   "He calls
it a 'short stay,'— I don't see that.
We were rarely longer at any port;
and no doubt Mat will put enough
into that blessed fortnight to last
him for a lifelong memory.   'Twill
be something to look back upon all
his days."

"But *we* are to see nothing of it,"
said Ernestine, bitterly.   "And he
wrote that he hoped to 'join our
party,' and would 'help to escort his
fair   cousins.'   How   mean   and
shabby he will think us!   How
amazed and disgusted he will be!"

"Can't help that, my girl;" the
captain, whose pipe was now alight,

smoked in affected unconcern which hid, as it was meant to do, a not inconsiderable share of his own perturbation. He did not mean to give in; and the best armour in which he could encase this resolution was that of outward indifference. Let Nesta once perceive that he was vulnerable on the point of supposed meanness, that he dreaded confessing to his prosperous nephew the scantiness of resources which compelled him to forego witnessing the Royal Procession, and she would certainly take advantage of his weakness. Happily she had some pride; she could be depended upon not to let fall the slightest hint which could be construed into an appeal, when Mat, the Australian, turned up; but she would give her own people no peace. He must hold her at bay.

Accordingly, he smoked either in silence or with an occasional sarcasm which had all the effect he could have hoped. The beauty was in tears at last, tears of mortification and anger.

"If he even minded, it would not seem so cruel," sobbed she to Molly, recounting the interview, "but father is so hard-hearted. One would think he had never been young and—and pretty."

Molly laughed at her; turned the joke against her; finally gave her one gentle, positive assurance that the thing could not be done—and a sudden sigh escaped as she spoke.

"I know you care," quoth Nesta, slightly mollified, "you have been thinking and thinking of it as well as I. What I thought was, if we two could have gone, and Mat with us—"

"It would have been nice, awfully nice. He would have known so much about it. And he would have told us who the big people were; and we would have cheered his Colonials."

"And we would have worn our white hats and frocks," Ernestine shook her brown curls sorrowfully. "We have been keeping them for this all along. And, Molly, what vexes me more than anything is that all those Miller girls, every single one of them, is going; they have had their seats for ever so long in the Borough; not the best, of course; but as good as any of their set have got, and I did think father could have afforded us the same. Two guineas each is not so very much; and if Mat——"

"I doubt if Mat would be content with those seats," quoth Molly, shrewdly.

"Oh," said her sister. Ernestine, for all her experience in St. George's Square, was not as wise in the world's ways as the keener-witted, more observant girl by her side.

"I think you are wrong," she said, however, after a minute's pause.

"Any one would be willing to do what the Millers do; they know what's what; and if we had a chance of seats in the Borough—"

"Of course we would jump at them. My dear, who am I, or who are you, to turn up our noses at seats in the gutter, let alone the Borough, if they came in our way? But the thing is, Nett, that we haven't the money. We have not got it;" very emphatically. "It isn't only the seats, there would be the train tickets both ways; and we should have to sleep in town, and the getting to our places—what are the Millers doing about that?" she inquired, suddenly.

"They are breakfasting at five, and are to be in their room by six o'clock," owned Nesta, reluctantly. "They have made out the whole thing, and kept talking about it before me all the time I was there on Thursday. When I said we had nothing arranged, they looked at each other, and Ethel and Annie exclaimed both at once: 'You poor things!' I said something about our running up for the day, and you should have seen Aunt Jessie's face. Oh, of course, we should have to sleep in London."

"There, you see!"

"All the same, it is too bad. We are not as poor as hundreds of people who are going; those dreadful little Spratts have seats in St. James's Palace, think of it! St. James's Palace! No one knows how they got them; but I suppose through some of the servants. And Margaret Robsen is to be at the War Office; and it seems as if everybody could get in *somewhere* except ourselves," tears again rising, "it will seem to Mat as if only his relations of all the people in England could not crawl into a corner to see the great Jubilee Procession."

Molly turned away without speaking. She felt as if for once her sister, the sister who often talked so foolishly and irrelevantly, were in the right.

"Is there no way in which it could be managed?" was now Nesta's cry, recurred to at shorter and shorter intervals. The poor girl really suffered; and there was nothing to distract her thoughts, for every one who came to Purfoy Farm was full of the one theme, and she had to hear its changes rung from every point of view.

"The thing is growing into a perfect nuisance!" muttered Captain Butterworth at last.

Only Molly felt for and with Ernestine. "It is hard to be so pretty and bright, and feel that she could enjoy everything so much, and that perhaps Mat would admire her and fall in love with her; oh, what nonsense I am talking!" cried the

little homely sister, blushing at herself, "but I do think Nett has more
to be said for her than father and
mother imagine. They cannot
enter into a girl's feelings. They
do not even see, because I don't
grumble aloud as poor Nesta does,
that I am in my heart hankering
after the fun too. I don't know
when I have cared about anything
so much."

This "caring" of her sister was in
truth Ernestine's only consolation.
The two for once felt alike, and drew
together in a common grief. Instead of going to bed each apart in
her own little chamber, Nesta half-
shyly at first, more confidently afterwards, was heard to tap at Molly's
door, and, brush in hand, suggest
that the night was too hot for bed all
at once, and that the two might talk
for a while in Molly's little dormer
window which stood open. Perhaps
it was these talks which drew from

Molly that gentle defence of her sister and those excuses which at once exasperated her father and moved him to admiration. "If that isn't the sweetest little nature in the whole world!" he would exclaim. But he found Ernestine more and more "difficult."

.   .   .   .

" 'Pon my word, you don't deserve it!" But pleasure shone in Captain Butterworth's eyes as he hurried up from the small gate of his domain with an open telegram in his hand. "Here, you monkey," throwing it to his younger daughter, and still keeping up a pretence of high disdain, "here's your precious Jubilee seat come at last. You have worried for it enough in all conscience."

"Oh, father—father, it really is! Mother, do you hear?" Nesta with blazing blue orbs turned to one and the other in her ecstasy of exultation. "And to go with them—the

Millers—and sleep at their house both nights and perhaps longer! Oh, how good, how kind! Dear Aunt Jessie! Molly," as Molly, attracted by the outcry, came flying up, "Molly, dear, only hear the news; Aunt Jessie has sent for one of us" —on a sudden the speaker's voice stopped short as though it had seen a ghost.

Molly, however, perceived nothing.

"For the Jubilee?" cried she, in answering excitement. "Oh, how glorious, how delightful! Let me see the telegram. Why, it is to go up this afternoon! Father, we must send to Surrey's about the pony-cart at once. I can go. Only," she paused. "I ought to help you with your packing, Nett. But if you could run up now, and put out your things, I could be back in time to do the rest. The 5:30 train will do. Is there any answer, father?"

"Answer went straight away, my lass. Your old dad knew what it would be. There was no need to consult you this time, and the reply was pre-paid."

"What did you say?" demanded Ernestine, in rather a low voice.

"Say? Said 'All right, and many thanks.' Short and sweet. There was nothing more wanted."

"You—you did not say which daughter?"

"Which daughter? Nay, there is no need for that," the captain laughed. "No need to tell the Millers, or any one who knows this house, which daughter gets all the good things."

Ernestine hastily left the room.

"Eh?" said the captain, opening his eyes. "She felt that, did she? But 'tis as well she should hear it for once, poor child. And maybe she will think of it even in her fine Jubilee seat."

"Father, don't be hard; dear father, you do not mean it, but that was a cruel thought. Nesta is not so selfish as you think; she is only——"

"Look here, Moll, truth is truth. Was there ever any question either with Nesta herself or with any single one of us who should be the person to accept your aunt's invitation? You are the elder. The telegram says 'One of your daughters,' yet no one for a moment hesitated between the two. That speaks for itself, my girl," as there ensued a pause during which Molly hung her head in silence. "However, I'll say no more," pursued her father, "and to be sure, I dare say the Millers meant Nesta, though they would not pass you over. And now that she has got her way, she will be more peaceable; for I dare say it has fretted her a bit, being as she is a pretty creature—at least, so folks tell me"—and he rambled on.

Molly was half-way across the fields, ere he had said his say for the time being.

The day was broiling, and the ground heavy from recent thundery rain (we all remember how unsettled was the weather during that tumultuous Jubilee week), so that it took the willing little messenger longer than she had expected to reach the village inn, whence a pony-cart could be hired, and by the time she had hurried back across the miry field-path, Molly expected to find an expectant head prospecting from Nesta's bedroom window; but no head was there. "She is too happy to be impatient," concluded the sister, "and I can pack while she dresses. There is plenty of time."

Accordingly she pattered upstairs, taking off her hat as she went, and thankful for the shade within the cool farmhouse; and there on the landing was Nesta, and——

"Hush!" said a voice, Nesta's
voice, but suppressed in a strange
fashion, "come in here, quick; I have
got everything ready, and you are
not to say a word."

The door closed, and we will not
open it to spy.

.   .   .   .   .   .

"Heyday, what's this?" the old
captain opened his mouth and shut
it again, confounded beyond the
power of speech.   He was standing
in the porch, the pony-cart was at
the door, and the luggage was in.
But the traveller—who—who was
the traveller?

"Oh, father, dear, she would make
me go; father, I could not help it;
I begged and prayed, and all Nesta
would say was——"

"Never mind what Nesta said."
Nesta was busy tucking a bunch of
roses into the pretty shirt front
which was her own, yet now peep-
ing   from   Molly's   little   coat.

"There, doesn't she look nice? Let mother see you, Mollkins, and I will run for a glass of milk, for I know you can't eat;" and she vanished.

"Shiver my timbers!" exclaimed the captain, nailed to the spot.

Molly it was who was trembling all over, as deeply ashamed and remorseful as though detected in a crime, scarcely even yet to be forced into compliance. "Father—mother —she would not let me ask you, she would not even let me tell you. Everything was ready when I went upstairs; she would put in all her own best things that she thought I would want; and she was so dear and kind," an irrepressible sob, the father turned his head and whistled softly, the mother's eyes glistened— "what could I do?" proceeded the criminal (she really felt herself to be one), "she hustled me into my clothes, and did my hair herself."

"Now, then, time's up!"—a gay

reminder from the doorway. "Drink, sister mine, and be off! Happiness go with you!"—an affectionate kiss. No one was supposed to see that Nesta's eyes were moist or that there was any suspicious redness in the lids.

"Really, father, she must go; you know how full the train will be!" And all in a bustle, poor Molly, still in a kind of dream, was swept from the door.

Captain Butterworth took one stride up to his remaining daughter and held out a sunburnt hand. Not a word did he say, but its grasp and the look and nod by which it was accompanied were felt to the girl's inmost soul.

She would not allow herself to feel dull when the excitement was over.

"If Moll is taking my place, I have got to take hers." And in and out went the light figure—Nesta here, Nesta there—no one had ever known

Nesta so busy and so cheerful—until at last there came a pause in household tasks, and from the lower garden, among the sweet peas and mignonette, there rose into the pure evening air the sound of a woman's singing.

"I scarcely expected to find any of my fair cousins at home!"

An unmistakable arrival had taken place. Day after day the inmates of Purfoy Farm had hoped to see their expected relation appear from the Antipodes, until at last it became so obvious that something had happened to delay his journey that the sisters had come almost to hope—it might be selfishly, but they could not help it—that he would not appear upon the scene till Jubilee Day was over.

"At least we may be spared that!" Nesta had sighed, with doleful resignation.

But now here was Mat, and it was

only Jubilee Eve. Her heart, in
spite of a sudden thump, sank a
little.

It was something, however, that
one of them should have gone, and,
Molly being the elder, all would
seem natural; and—and she had on
a clean sprigged muslin, ready for
anything that might turn up (it had
been donned on purpose to show to
all whom it might concern that Nesta
was not moping). So, putting a
brave front upon it, up she rose from
the strawberry-bed, over which she
had been stooping, and—

"How do you do, Cousin Mat?"
said she, readily. "We have been
expecting you for ever so long!"

Expecting him, had she? "Faith,"
thought Mat Butterworth to himself, "if I had known I was being
'expected,' and by such a goddess!"
And he sat down in the rose-arbour
by Ernestine's side.

"She has told you all about it, I

suppose," said the old captain, strolling down to call them in presently.
"My word, those Jubilee seats!
Swindles, that's what I call them!   I
hope, nephew, I do hope you have
not been let in for anything out-
rageous; though, · of course, you
know your own business best.   But
five, ten, fifteen guineas—anything
you like to name—is the order of
the day.   And for what?   Eighteen
inches of hard board!   And there
you have to sit frying in dust and
heat!—"

"Certainly, it is a vast deal pleasanter here," said the young man,
frankly.   And, being of an open
nature and bred to straightforward
dealing, he saw no harm in adding
presently, "I am fortunate, uncle,
to find one of my cousins at home;
and though, no doubt, she would
rather be in London——"

"She let Molly go," said Captain
Butterworth, quickly.   "What?   Am

not I to say it? Oh, but it's only fair! It was between them, d'ye see. And, poor things, they were both simply off their heads to go; but—well, well, I say no more. What about yourself, Mat? Are you off to-night, or will the morning train do for you?"

"Certainly not to-night. Yes, yes, the morning; any morning train will do."

The captain stared. "'Any' morning train! What are you thinking of, young man? If you don't start before break of day——"

"I have my seat, you know, sir."

"You have? And a good one, I'll be bound. But how are you going to get to it? That's the point. If it's in the Borough——"

"It is not in the Borough."

"Humph, the Strand, then? Or Fleet Street? The cram will be still worse in Fleet Street or the Strand."

"It is in a corner window of Piccadilly looking down St. James's Street," said Mat, the colour suffusing his brown cheek, for he had meant to keep this back if he could. "So, you see, any time will do."

"Fifteen or twenty guineas, eh?" The captain swallowed something in his throat. "And you seem as indifferent about getting there——"

"I am indifferent."

Now, how was it that, though Nesta was looking the other way, she not only heard an underlying meaning in the accents, but knew that a certain pair of dark eyes were turned full upon her face and rested there while her cousin spoke? She twisted off a moss-rose and smelt it.

"I am so jolly indifferent," continued the bronzed Australian, deliberately, "that I doubt very much if I shall take the trouble to attempt it. Why should I? You are not going, my aunt is not going"—a pause, then—"and Ernestine is not going," concluded the speaker, softly.

After the evening meal, he asked Ernestine to go out again with him. Why not? She was his cousin; and, besides, if a man is not to have a girl to himself, how can he tell whether the pretty face be nothing but a pretty face, or whether the dawnings of a deeper feeling than mere admiration within his bosom may dare expand into maturity?

Round and round the little gravelled garden the two sauntered in the scented dusk.

"I wonder whether I did not dream of something like this," said Mat, at last. "I think if I had found you all agog for the Jubilee with its fun and fume, I should have been almost disappointed. At least, it seems so to me now. Of course, I hope your sister will enjoy herself, and I am sure she will; but I am so glad she went, and"—again the softer, more significant note—"so very glad you let her go."

Poor Nesta had never felt so much ashamed and yet so happy in her life. It was of no avail to stammer out a confused explanation which only served to show her to more advantage than ever in her companion's eyes. She had to accept his homage and his obvious conviction of her unselfish character, and inwardly resolve that, in the future, she would try to deserve it.

"And you are not going up at all?"

It was perfectly incredible to Captain Butterworth that a man who had paid twenty guineas for his seat should not go near it when, moreover, there was not even a chance of getting his money back; but it appeared that this was his strange nephew's intention. Mat had made up his mind in the night. The idea of Ernestine wandering lonely among her sweet peas, of leaving her behind in however sweet a spot while he ruffled it among grandees in his costly place at the great Jubilee show, was not to be borne.

"If I could have taken her with me!" he thought; but that could not, of course, be done.

"Then, here goes!" cried Mat Butterworth, and tore up his ticket into small pieces.

Space forbids us to tell how that long summer day passed for him and for Ernestine. Wherever she went, there went he. Whatever duties and occupations she engaged in, he shared. She showed him her favourite walk; and they sat together in a shady nook by a bubbling stream at the very hour when, had things fallen out otherwise, each would have been differently ensconced, "And not together," as Mat significantly observed.

He pulled out his watch and told
her exactly what would be passing as
the moments flew by; he hoped Molly
would be able to remember and tell
him if his conjectures were correct.
He did not seem at all to mind when
a new telegram arrived—this time
from Molly herself—to the effect
that, as the party durst not venture
forth to see the illuminations the
same night, the crowd being too
great, her aunt insisted on keeping
her till Thursday.   As for Nesta?
Nesta was almost frightened to feel
as she did.   That telegram was like
a reprieve.

So the next day it was the same
thing over again; and by evening
Nesta had learned all about her
cousin's home-life in that far land,
perceived that, in spite of his wealth
and the luxury in which he lived, he
was a solitary man with starved
affections, and a large heart longing
to be filled; and scarce daring to

believe it was so, yet had a conviction which thrilled every vein,
namely, that he had already decided
who could fill it.

"Seems to me you didn't lose so
much through giving up your
Jubilee seat after all," said the old
captain, when they told him.

THOSE SORT OF PEOPLE

Those Sort of People

***

"I really cannot see why you should be so set upon going *there*," said Mrs. Boscastle, with a contemptuous intonation on the last word, which directly indicated its status. "You have been determined about it from the very first. I never knew you so obstinate about anything." She paused, but as there was no response, took up the theme with renewed animation. "It is not as if you were always so particular about engagements. I am sure I wish you were. When you are asked to other houses—when 'Miss Boscastle' is distinctly mentioned beneath your father's and my name—as often as not you insist on Mary's going."

"Only in fair turn, mamma. 'Miss Boscastle' on an ordinary card means either of us. In this case it does not—as you know."

"Oh, I know; I know very well. Those sort of people must always have the best. They want to show you off, of course."

An impatient movement, but the speaker either did not or would not perceive it. "A tea party in West Kensington!" Again the disdainful inflection, this time, if possible, more accentuated than before. "In West Kensington! In Shepherd's Bush, I suppose, if the truth were told. In a little semi-detached villa facing the green, I dare say. It is too absurd to give up Ranelagh on a lovely June afternoon for such a wretched, such an absolutely squalid entertainment."

"You would have had me say this?"

"Edith, don't be ridiculous. And there is no need to get angry over it. If you had done as I told you to do at the first, accepted *condition- ally*—agreed to go if nothing prevented you——"

"If nothing better turned up."

"Precisely. You would have meant that, and they would have understood it, and it would have been as much as they could have expected. You know I am quite glad—ahem! I entirely approve of your affection for your old governess ——," Edith Boscastle raised her eyes, and her step-mother proceeded somewhat hurriedly, "It is all right and proper; Miss Peters was an excellent instructress, who deserved all the esteem you could give her; but, having ceased to have any connection with this house professionally, I must say I think it rather a pity—that is to say, we are always glad to see her here, without there being any occasion for your going among her people."

"This is the first time she has ever asked it; and she inquired privately of you, if either papa or you would have any objection, before she mentioned the subject to me."

"She did, very properly. And if only it had not been for a Saturday, and we had not had Ranelagh tickets——"

"That need not matter, surely. You will take Mary; and Mary would greatly like to go."

Mrs. Boscastle fidgeted. What she longed to say, and did not dare to say, was, that while her plainer step-daughter would make no sensation, attract no admiring glances from the gay crowds in the haunt of fashion, she would have been perfectly good enough for the suburban studio, on which it was a shame to waste her sister. Debarred from giving vent to the sentiment, she could only feebly return to her first charge. "I could not have believed you would be so tiresome, Edith."

Now Edith Boscastle was a wise girl; she did not attempt to argue the point. To have done so would have been to inflame opposition, and opposition occasionally led to a battle-royal in the doctor's house, subsequent to which peace would only be restored by giving up the point at issue. This she did not mean to do.

In her heart of hearts she not only felt the full force of her step-mother's argument, but it was backed up by a secret consciousness which had already caused more than one sigh to escape since the arrival of the coveted tickets. Some one had sent them—some one whom Edith liked very much indeed.

Under other circumstances she would have flown to her chamber to don her prettiest dress and hat, and joyful anticipation would have painted a tint upon her cheek, and sparkle in her eye; but disappoint her poor, dear, humble little friend who had so long before arranged the day and hour, talked of it, planned for it, and whose preparations were doubtless now complete? She could not do this.

She had herself named a Saturday as being usually a free day; and the present Saturday had been absolutely barren of engagements three weeks before, at which time the quondam governess made her modest appeal. An artist brother (married, and entirely unobjectionable, as Mrs. Boscastle took care to note) was setting up his small studio on the outskirts of London, and having brought with him from abroad a collection of pictures and sketches, fancied it would be to him something of the coveted "start" so important in every career, if these could be viewed by friends likely

either to become themselves patrons,
or to interest others more artistically
disposed.

It was an acknowledged fact that
no one could interest the head of the
house in Harley Street as could the
eldest daughter.

"We thought perhaps if *you* would
come, Edith?" said Jane Peters,
wistfully; and neither Edith nor any
one else wondered why the speaker
said *you*.

So that, on the whole, it was
manifestly unfair in Mrs. Boscastle
to profess a species of ignorance
which could only be sheltered beneath insinuations totally wide of the
mark, and yet unanswerable; because
the girl who was both prettier and
wittier than her sister could no more
have alleged, "I am wanted because
my father thinks more of one word
from me than of a thousand from
Mary," than she could have protested, "You, on your part, want me

because I reflect credit on you by my appearance, and Mary does not."

Nothing could be said openly, and she was obliged to trust to her step-mother's good taste and good feeling prevailing in the long run. Taste perhaps would hardly have effected much in Mrs. Boscastle's case, but she had, with all her defects—and they were patent to the dullest intelligence—heart enough to make her just stop short of giving pain to the simple girl who was so ready to acknowledge herself her sister's inferior, and so affectionately proud of the fact.

"Mary does not mind," Mrs. Boscastle would exclaim, with easy indifference. "Mary is a good girl, and of course she can't help seeing." On ordinary occasions she would herself be touched by Mary's ready acquiescence in any putting forward of the show member of the family. (We may be sure from whom this idea emanated.) The lady would be touched and pleased, we say, and in high good humour would pat poor Mary's cheek for a "dear, unselfish creature," assuring her moreover that looks were nothing, and that many of the best marriages were made by the plainest girls. If the cheek flushed a little beneath such consolation, Mary's step-mother never saw it.

She was kind to both the girls in her way. Luckily for them, and perhaps for herself, she had no children of her own, and they were thus able to retain through subsequent years the place they had been accorded in her estimation, when in the first gush of her marriage prosperity she had swallowed with joy anything and anybody connected with the elderly widower whose proposals secured her future comfort and independence. Previously she had earned her own living, and a hard and precarious livelihood it had been.

Accordingly, the two little ones who constituted Dr. Boscastle's sole family were hardly felt to be even in the way—she would have accepted him if there had been a dozen of them—and as the elder of the two bloomed and budded into lovely maidenhood, and as both were docile under her rule—had no spite against her—no desire to throw off her yoke—did not even seek to jostle her aside as she saw others with the genuine claim of motherhood jostled— she grew to entertain a warmer feeling towards them both than pupils who had known her in her capacity of governess could have believed possible.

In Edith her pride might be centred; but where vanity and social ambition did not bar the way, there was as much, if not positively more, affection for Mary.

Pride and social ambition—those two ever-green demons—did, however, not infrequently rumple up the waves when otherwise all might have been smooth sailing between the three with whom our little story is most concerned. Mrs. Boscastle could not look at Edith without noting the elegance of her shape, the pose of her head, and the delicate curves of her chin and brow. She was forever making comparisons between her and others of her age and sex. She watched them go out and in, took stock of their clothes, their movements, their manners and affectations. She did not like it if a young visitor were taller or smarter.

In her own mind the conviction was assured that Edith at her best, in lively spirits and becoming raiment, could out-distance any of her peers; but she knew that it behoved Edith to be at her best. It was therefore imperative that she should go into public of her own accord, gladly and willingly—not to be dragged thither because Mrs. Boscastle would not go without her.

It was also necessary to let her alone when there; to permit her to talk to whom she chose, walk or sit, as she preferred. Edith's step-mother made quite a study of her charge during the first year after she "came out" and at the end of that year she fully expected never to have another of the kind.

"I shall have no such credit in poor Mary," she sighed, in doleful prediction,—but she was not as well content as she might have been to find that although "poor Mary" was ready to step on the stage, the stage was not cleared for her, as prophets united in foretelling it would be. The beautiful Edith was still on hand.

So that now, in the middle of Edith's second London season, little

scenes such as we have hearkened to
above were not altogether infrequent
in the doctor's house, and it only
remains to say one thing more.
Although Edith Boscastle had her
own reason for finding the path of
fidelity and kindness a hard one to
tread on in the day in question, she
would sooner have died than confided this to her step-mother. There
was plenty of goodwill but no real
sympathy between natures so opposite.

. ` . . . .

"Do you think she will come?"
said Mr. Harold Peters, in his thin,
nervous voice. He had been ham-
mering and hanging, and wearing
himself out ever since morning in
the little, hot double-room now
turned into a picture-gallery.
"Young ladies are so forgetful."

"Edith will not forget. She is as
true as steel," asserted Edith's
sponsor, confidently; "when she was

in the schoolroom, if she promised to do a thing she would do it, though a thousand lions stood in the path."

"Lions? Oh, well, we hardly run to 'lions' in West Kensington; I wish we did." The artist laughed a feeble, high-pitched, anxious little pretence of a laugh. "Even one lion would be a 'draw' worth any money to us at the present moment. But this ex-pupil of yours—you speak as if she were rather a determined, dare-devil sort of character, eh? Suppose she takes a wrong turn? Suppose she is in a carping, fault-finding humour? Suppose——"

"Nay, dear brother, with idle suppositions we need not cumber ourselves. Real facts are hard enough to deal with." The gentle creature heaved a patient sigh. "We have been successful so far," she continued, more briskly. "Everybody has been kind in promising to come

to-day; the weather is cool and
fresh outside, though our little house
is rather warm; as for the tea and
strawberries"—looking complacently
at a small set-out, which had been
arranged with care, and sent forth
a delicious odour, tempting to the
most jaded palate. "Grace has
surpassed herself," continued the
speaker, smiling round at another
slight, colourless figure which glided
forward from back regions at the
moment.

It was characteristic of all three
that they spoke in muffled tones, and
moved as afraid of free, unre-
strained action. With many tremors
they had approached this day in
their lives which meant to them a
crisis.

And one of the three, she who
had boldly conceived the project and
thrown her whole soul into it, had
to keep to herself the trump card
with which her sleeve was trembling!

She had it there; now and then it almost peeped out; had there been a Harold without his Grace, or a Grace without her Harold, it must have been produced in moments of dire secrecy,—but stickler as she was for absolute confidence between husband and wife, how could she expect aught than that a discovery upon which she had alit by sheerest accident, but which might now be turned to rare account, would not have been the subject of conversation and conjecture between the fond pair?

This was not to be borne. Her dear Edith's name was not to be bandied about by strangers, even with no ill intent; and no one guessed that the staunch espouser of the brother's cause and prophetess of his fame, had a little wire to pull on her own account, which' no other fingers must presume to touch.

"Lady Victoria Swallowfield!"

Good gracious! Her ladyship to be the first to arrive, and no one to hear her announced!

This, it must be confessed, was the first thought which sent a thrill of disappointment through the breast of the artist's poor little wife.

Possibly it was a vulgar thought, but Grace was but a homely tradesman's daughter, and she had never spoken to a "Lady" Anybody in her life. And she had counted, poor soul, on the sensation in her little room when the door should open to admit such a guest, and on the faces of the others when Jane should go forward in her quiet, composed manner to receive her own especial friend.

Jane would show nothing. She might feel the honour, perhaps she might even murmur her sense of it into Lady Victoria's ear,—but outwardly, she would be as calm as if such an event were of everyday occurrence.

Harold and his wife had been
assured when in doubts as to the
propriety of sending an invitation to
the stately dame of quality, that
Jane would see them through,—and
with that rod on which to lean,
they had been able to bear the
anticipation.

But here was the terrible moment,
with all its pangs and none of its
sweets! She felt the ill-luck to the
bottom of her soul.

She did her best, however; and
those who knew Lady Victoria
would have told her that this august
personage was unusually gracious.
Ordinarily there was an atmosphere
surrounding her ladyship in which
it was not easy to breathe. She was
shy, she was proud, she had a repel-
lent manner, and a poker back.
Even when most pleased to meet a
neighbour or acquaintance, the
slowly extended fingers and the
frigid greeting made cordiality diffi-

cult on the part of the recipient.
She would say, "I am so glad to see
you," in tones that would more
fittingly have expressed, "I wish
you were at the other end of the
earth."

But beneath the crust there were
those who knew that a true heart
beat, and that once admitted to
Lady Victoria's esteem, the place
was held in perpetuity. Jane
Peters, when begging the favour of
her kind friend's presence at the
studio, had faithfully delineated its
locality, and prepared her for its
insignificance,—and Jane knew that
she could not better have secured
her object than by such a course.
Benevolence now softened a countenance usually severe.

The one large chair in the room
had been placed in its coolest part,
and through the little window at the
back a faint breeze fanned a meagre
tree-top. "I am so thankful to get

into this pleasant shade," said Lady Victoria, cheerfully.

"How splendid she looks!" thought Grace Peters, from afar. "All that black silk and lace—so effective! And I am glad her ladyship is stout; somehow it makes so much *more* of her than if she were a thin woman. No one can help seeing her—even if she did come rather soon for her name to be heard."

Jane, too, took occasion to whisper that Lady Victoria was not going to hurry away. Lady Victoria would not have her tea just yet; she would like to sit and chat a while; and then go round the pictures and see the portfolio, and be ready for tea when others came in.

"So they will all see the carriage at the door," thought Grace.

She could not resist a peep outside, as she stood nervously by her teapots, there being nothing for her

to do the while Jane composedly conversed with the guest, and Harold
hovered near, waiting the right
moment for Art to be appealed to.

The big barouche, with its glitter-
ing harness and champing horses,
gave an air to the whole neighbourhood. It seemed a shame that it
should have to move aside presently, even for the very good little
brougham with its glossy chestnut,
which was the next arrival.

· And more vehicles followed.
People whom Grace had certainly
expected to appear either on foot,
or at best in cabs and hansoms,
turned up in well-appointed equip-
ages, with smart liveried servants on
their box-seats—so that by the time
the apartment within was full (and
it held more than could have been
supposed), there was quite a festive
little crowd in front, and the success of Mr. Peters' studio tea was
assured.

Last of all to arrive was Miss Edith Boscastle. In she came, blushing like a rose, and looking very like a rose altogether in her freshest and fairest dress, all eagerness to explain a delay which must not be allowed to appear of set purpose, especially since there could be no mistaking the pause which made her silver tones audible on every side.

"How horrible! It looks as if I meant to make a grand *entrée!*" cried she to herself.

And she had tried to be there an hour before, and it was pure accident which had hindered her, and caused the sensation of the hour!

The sensation penetrated to the innermost recesses of the back room where Lady Victoria Swallowfield still clung to her big chair, though she was now contentedly sipping tea and munching cake. She had

accomplished the purpose for which
she had come; admired and praised
and given a handsome order;
furthermore, she had promised to
speak to her brother, the duke, who
was on the point of having his largest country seat newly decorated,
and had spoken about frescoes on the
walls—(Harold's breath went and
came as he listened)—Lady Victoria
thought, yes, she certainly thought
the duke would give attention to her
recommendation, however he might
eventually decide. She could, of
course, promise nothing,—but there
was enough without the promise
to make the poor artist's eyes
kindle.

Business done, the old lady enjoyed her tea, and at the moment of
Edith Boscastle's appearance on the
scene was hearkening favourably to
a suggestion of strawberries; but
somehow—and she remembered this
afterwards with satisfaction, for her

doctor might have looked grave—she never got the strawberries.

"Who is that?" she exclaimed, suddenly. "What name did you say, my dear?"

Jane Peters, who was never very far from her ladyship's chair, bent over the speaker in a moment. Edith had been in the room for about ten minutes.

"A former pupil of yours? I did not know that. I never heard you mention the Boscastles."

Jane was silent. It had not been her business to mention the Boscastles.

"She is certainly a very pretty girl," murmured Lady Victoria, scanning through her eyeglass the light figure in its rosebud draperies.

"She is as good as she is pretty," said Miss Peters, in a low, distinct, emphatic voice. She was pulling her wire now.

The old lady dropped her eyeglass with a jerk, and turned round as though surprised. "Good, did you say? Good, Jane? And you speak from knowledge, of course. Your position would enable you to judge. But I thought, I certainly both thought and heard that these Boscastles——" she moved uneasily in her chair.

"Edith ought not to be confounded with her step-mother, Lady Victoria. She ought not to make one when you talk of 'these Boscastles.' Not that it is for me to say a word against Mrs. Boscastle, who was always kind to me, but——"

"I understand; I understand. A forward, pushing woman. And wild to be taken up by society—to fly in at every open door. They tell me she is determined to marry off those girls, and hawks them about in the most barefaced manner. I am old-fashioned and strict in my

notions, I suppose; but I must confess that ever since my son took to
visiting at the Boscastles' I have
worried over his being so intimate
with people of whom I disliked
everything I ever heard."

The governess was wisely silent.

"But she certainly has a sweet
face!" said Lady Victoria, slowly
raising the eyeglass a second time.

After a moment she beckoned
down Jane's ear again. "How
comes it that she is here to-day? I
know my son expected to meet her
at Ranelagh. He sent them tickets;
I was annoyed with him for doing
so. And Jane—oh, I wish I could
speak to you alone—it is so difficult,
young men are so tiresome to manage, and he says he is not a young
man now. Jane, I *wish* you would
tell me what you think." (No wonder strawberries and cream vanished
from her ladyship's thoughts.) "I
had no idea *you* could help me," she

murmured at last, almost reproach-
fully.

"Dear Lady Victoria, my help
would be to bring up Edith, and let
you judge her for yourself."

"It could do no harm, could it?
And Victor would be pleased. And
she does look—she really has a
charming face" (eyeglass again in
requisition). "Yes, I think I should
like to speak to her; but one word,
Jane, before you go. Did she know
I was coming? Did you talk it over
with her? Was there any scheme?—
Oh, dear, what am I saying? Forgive me, my dear, I did not mean to
be rude and stupid; and of course
you—I could trust you anywhere.
All I want is to know whether
she——"

"Was absolutely ignorant of my
having even invited you, Lady Victoria. It is not my place to tattle of
the friendship with which you honour
me; and I do not see Edith often

enough to make the mention of your
name spontaneous. This dear, *kind*
girl gave up her own pleasure and
toiled out all this way to-day, purely
from the same motive that you did
yourself.''

Lady Victoria pressed the hand
which lay on the arm of her chair.
Her ear, albeit by no means a quick
one, caught a falter of emotion in
the words which appealed at once to
her best impulses.

"I gave up nothing, Jane. I had
no gay parties waiting for me; no
gallant admirer — ahem! — Jane,
could *you* have done it? He may
take it amiss, you know. Men are
so tiresome and foolish; and a man
in love—oh, you are discretion itself
—you will never repeat. I can tell
you that Victor is in love, desper-
ately in love, with this girl, and will
not hear a word against her. And I
have been so put out and worried;
for the idea certainly is that—I

hardly like to suggest it of that innocent-looking creature—but they do tell me she is throwing herself, or being thrown, at my son's head."

" 'Being thrown,' Lady Victoria, possibly! 'Throwing herself?' Never. One has but to know Edith Boscastle—"

"Then let me know her," quoth Lady Victoria, cutting the matter short.

"And now to pull wire No. 2," nodded Jane Peters to herself, as she threaded her way through the talking, tea-drinking assemblage. (She noted how brisk the chatter was, and how well everything was going, as she did so.) "Now, poor Edith, for your start and shock!"

But there was neither start nor shock.

Edith had long before descried the black figure in the large armchair, and recognised it.

Of course she did; of course she

quailed before such an apparition!
How strange, how extraordinary, to
meet it here! To run across Victor
Swallowfield's proud, impenetrable
mother, who was supposed never to
go anywhere—never, at least, to any
ordinary house, and whom Mrs.
Boscastle had in vain hoped to meet
at any public or private entertainment—to find her in this dingy little
dwelling, in this back-of-beyond
neighbourhood!

And how peaceful the great lady
looked, sitting well back in her
comfortable chair, placidly bearing
her prominent part in the festivity.
—[N. B.—This was before she saw
Edith. Edith, as we know, had
been present for some small space of
time ere the vision of her, decked in
all the charms of youth and beauty,
so moved Lady Victoria that she
inquired of Jane Peters, "Who is
she?"]—Subsequently no one could
have said that either the old face or

figure looked "placid." The face worked strangely, the figure moved incessantly.

The truth was that Fate, whimsical Fate, had pierced between joints of armour already rattling. Lady Victoria had had a bad night, followed by an unhappy morning. Her only son, the darling of her heart, had defied her,—and if that defiance were to last and she could not find some means by which to break it down, she might as well give up the ghost at once. Whom had she on earth but Victor?

And now, Victor had told her plainly what he, shy and reticent as herself, had only permitted to be guessed before, that her worst fears respecting a family she disliked and disapproved were to be realised forthwith.

Victor was a proud man; he did not deign to say, "You misjudge Edith Boscastle; you are unfair

and prejudiced. You might trust
me to choose my own wife." Instead of this, he rather chuckled
inwardly, monster that he was, at
the thought of the triumph which
lay before him, supposing all went
well. His poor mother would strike
her colours on the instant. A single
interview would do it. But he
meanly withheld that interview.

The two had been really angry
with each other that morning; and
Lady Victoria, outwardly serene as
she appeared, was sore at heart as
she drove along the dusty, noisy
Uxbridge Road; and so—and so—no
wonder the fine old lady now shook
and trembled, her soul big with a
new purpose.

She rose and curtseyed as Edith
was led up to the arm-chair.

Then she took the small hand in
hers. "My dear," she said, and the
young girl was emboldened to raise
her eyes by the soft accents, "I

know you very well by name, and
perhaps you know me equally well.
My son——" A pause. A scarlet
blush on the remorselessly exposed
countenance before the speaker.

("It is all right," cried Lady Victoria to herself.)

And she needed no eyeglass to tell
her how becoming was the blush—
she must needs break off short, and
fly to the point at once. "He is
looking for you at Ranelagh to-day,
and you are here instead?" she murmured interrogatively.

"I could not help it, Lady
Victoria; I could not disappoint
them."

"Was that—forgive my asking it
—your *only* reason, Miss Boscastle?"

"Indeed it was," earnestly, almost
tearfully. "I—they—it was an old
engagement, and I knew they
cared,—it was not like an ordinary party,—it would have been
unkind, cruel, to throw them over.

Oh, *you* know, Lady Victoria. You would not have done it yourself."

Lady Victoria nodded, her eyes shining. Then she slowly rose from her chair, to hold out her hand anew. "Miss Boscastle, I have a proposal to make. My son invited you to Ranelagh to-day, and you did not go; will you come there with me now, because his mother does?"

. . . .

"Oh, Lady Victoria is carrying off Edith," said little Miss Peters, easily.